The Big Bike Mystery

Pauline Hutchens Wilson
Sandy Dengler

MOODY PRESS
CHICAGO

Library of Congress Cataloging-in-Publication Data

Wilson, Paulien Hutchens.
  The big bike mystery / Pauline Hutchens Wilson.
    p. cm. – (New Sugar Creek Gang ; 2)
  Summary: Eleven-year-old Les and his friends in the
New Sugar Creek Gang become involved in a case of
arson.
  ISBN 0-8024-8662-2
  [1. Arson–Fiction. 2. Christian life–Fiction. 3. Mystery
and detective stories.] I. Title.

PZ7. W69758 Bi 2001
[Fic]–dc21

                                              00-048702

1 3 5 7 9 10 8 6 4 2

Printed in the United States of America

INTRODUCTION

I t just isn't the same."

My dad sounded so sad. We stood on the walkway of a freeway overpass, looking out across a sea of new houses. Miles of houses, street after street.

"That line of trees out there is Sugar Creek." He waved an arm toward the hives of condos. "All this used to be farmland. When Paul Hutchens wrote those books about the Sugar Creek Gang, this is the area he wrote about. Right here."

I'm eleven, and, according to Dad, I'm older than most of the *homes* out here. "At least there's still a Sugar Creek," I said. "How far is it from our new place?"

"Couple miles. But the past—that was another world." He looked at me. "I'm sorry the fun is gone."

Dad walked down the slope to our car. I fell in behind him, wishing he didn't feel so sad.

When I was little, he read to me every night. And my favorite books to read were about a bunch of kids called the Sugar Creek Gang. They lived on farms near a creek and had a zillion adventures, mostly out in nature somewhere.

When Dad switched jobs, he found out we were going to move into the very area where the stories took place. He got all excited. I think he expected to find those farms here yet.

He grew up on a farm, so he knows a lot about that stuff. Every few pages, Dad would stop reading and say, "Now, Les, let me tell you about—" and then he'd explain something about spiders or shitepokes or whatever the story was talking about. So good old Les—that's me—learned a lot about farm life and nature when I was little, even though we lived in town.

We drove back to our brand-new home. It was an older house on a shady little back street. Just then it was full of boxes that the moving van had dumped the day before. And I mean full. Not very homey yet, but our beds were put together and made up, so who needs more?

Early next morning, I put on my jacket and found my helmet. It took me a while to dig my bike out of the garageful of jumbled stuff. Then I rode off, headed west.

So Dad thought the fun was gone. I wasn't so sure. That broad strip of trees along the creek looked awfully inviting.

I figured maybe I could find something interesting there. so that's how it all started.

I never guessed that I'd get all wrapped up in a real, true adventure like the ones we'd read about. And I would never *ever* have guessed that the Sugar Creek Gang would come back.

PAULINE HUTCHENS WILSON

1

Desperate to get away from the charging rhinoceros, the jungle adventurer grabbed a convenient vine and swung out over a river. Beneath him, a gigantic maw opened, bigger than any hippo's. He fired a pink laser gun. The thing sank back beneath the water, and the explorer landed safely on the far bank. Darting here and there, he ran through dense jungle toward safety.

"Rhinoceroses don't live in jungles," I complained. "They're plains animals. Open country." I was a lot of things just then: Les Walker, eleven years old, redheaded as all-get-out, on school vacation, and bored spitless by Bits's silly computer game.

The whole gang of us—the new Sugar Creek Gang, as we considered ourselves—had one thing in common. We all knew the old Sugar Creek books practically by heart. Not only that, we all lived within a couple miles of the original Sugar Creek. It was a county park now, with not a farm in sight, but that's progress.

No progress in that computer game, though. The five of us clustered around Bits's monitor in her dad's den. Bits had bragged about this game, so we all sat watching it in action. And I use the term *action* loosely. Slo-mo is closer to the truth.

"Who cares where rhinos live? It's a minor detail. Quit whining." Bits was Elizabeth Ware, my age, and totally taken by her game. Her brown ponytail bobbed when she hit the joystick fast.

Some people say it's not the big things in life that get you; it's the little ones that you think aren't much, such as where rhinos live. That afternoon proved that saying true, because if Bits's game had been more fun, we all would have just sat around watching and playing it. But it wasn't, and we didn't, so we helped out at an accident.

In addition to that, the Sugar Creek Gang launched out into a long string of goofy errors and excellent choices. Did it all come out OK? Let me tell you our story, and see what *you* think.

* * *

Scowling, Tiny wagged his head. "Look at the arc of his swing. A vine can't do that. The fulcrum's in the middle at the top, but his trajectory is nearly flat." His name was really Clarence Wilson, but everyone called him Tiny because he definitely was not. Tiny, that is. He was the tallest, lankiest kid in school, but I probably weighed more. Tiny was black, smart, an in-command kind of guy, and obviously just as bored as I was. "He'd have to grab the vine from second-story level to keep from getting his backside soaked. Even then it'd be close."

The action figure screeched to a halt. This huge male lion stood right in front of him. It didn't crouch. It just stood. And roared, a sound like someone's stomach growling. Then it waited patiently, motionless, while the hero drew his pink laser gun.

"Lions aren't jungle animals either. And all these problems with the graphics . . . *Jungle Peril* is supposed to be an educational game. Why are they teaching us so many wrong things?" Lynn, the logical one, was so soft-spoken that she sometimes didn't catch your attention. Her dad was Chinese, and her mom's grandparents came from Japan. "Traditional enemies, China and Japan," Lynn liked to say. "No wonder I'm confused." Don't let her kid you. There wasn't anybody less confused than Lynn Wing.

"And why a *pink* laser, for crying out loud?!" Little Mike Alvarado was a year-and-some younger than everyone else, but he kept up with us just fine, and sometimes was way ahead.

I asked, "Bits, did you freeze frame?"

"No. Why?"

"Then I guess it just seems that slow." I stood up.

Tiny stood up, too. "Where you going?"

"I dunno. Out into the real world, I guess."

"I'll go with you."

Lynn said, "Me too."

Mike stayed, because Bits promised he could

play the next round. Lynn and Tiny followed me out.

Bits's dad, mowing his lawn, saw us leave. He killed the mower. "Bits isn't going with you?"

"She and Mike are swatting tsetse flies."

He wagged his head. "Ride safely." And he torched off his mower again.

Lynn, Tiny, and I hopped on our bikes and left.

Tiny called, "Where to?"

From the back, Lynn called, "Sugar Creek?" And away we went.

We were approaching the corner of Elm and 24th when the accident happened, right in front of us.

A woman in a white Toyota blew through a stop sign and slammed into one of those little Ford Ranger pickup trucks. The two, all crunched together into a single wad, slid across the intersection into a power pole. Another car veered to avoid the pileup and hit a fire hydrant. We three bicyclists stopped barely in time to avoid becoming a part of all that.

I just sort of stood there, stunned. If I had spoken just then, it would have been babble, not words. Lynn pressed both hands to her mouth, aghast.

But good old Tiny knew exactly what to do. He threw down his bike and ran toward the pileup. He pointed to a scared-looking fellow with a cell phone in his hand. "Call 911, please! Tell them there are injuries."

How did he know that? Then I noticed the pickup driver had blood all over his face.

Tiny yelled, "Les! Lynn! Get the baby!" and pointed to the Toyota.

As Lynn and I ran to the car, Tiny was sending people here and there to direct traffic.

What a mess the Toyota was! The whole front end was smashed. The air bag had deployed, and the inside was cloudy with harsh, irritating powder. Someone who obviously knew first aid was tending to the mama at the wheel. And in the backseat, a baby in a car carrier howled.

Lynn tugged on the carrier while I fought the seat belt buckle. By the time we got the baby out, carrier and all, that air-bag powder had us hacking and coughing, too.

Uh-oh! "Wait, Lynn! Stand still!"

The power pole was tilted askew. I took a second to trace all the power lines up there. None of them had broken. Many a time, Dad had warned me never to get near downed wires. "It's OK. Let's go!"

Lynn and I moved way off to the side. Lynn held the wailing baby in its carrier. The mother was wailing loudly now, also, as the people attending her assured her the baby was fine. Someone else was trying to help the pickup driver, and lots of other people were crowding around, and you could smell gas a little, and you could smell hot antifreeze a lot, and you could smell that irritating powder that was still making Lynn, the baby, and me cough, and the whole world was churning and confusing.

After all that, I finally remembered. A smart person prays when everything goes bonkers. So I did, asking God to handle the injuries and everything else.

Then the aid van arrived with its own set of howling, piercing noises and flashing lights. Lynn and I handed the baby to a woman paramedic as she got out. She took it immediately into the back of the van.

Tiny joined us up on the curb. We tried to watch without getting in the way, but too many people milled around in front of us to see anything much.

"Know what?" Lynn said.

"What?" Tiny, being taller, could see better. He looked devastated.

"The real thing isn't anything at all like some computer game."

2

Some things in life are never meant to be. For example, elephants don't jump. They're built in such a way that they can't. Another example, dragonflies don't walk. They fly. They perch. They catch mosquitoes in midair. But they can't take a step.

And eleven-year-old boys with red hair don't go shopping. They simply do not. Trust me on this. So you can imagine the personal pain I suffered as I slogged along behind my mom and sisters at the Brookstone Mall for most of a morning.

We had just moved to this town from Seattle, Washington. That means we needed stuff for the new house that we either left behind or never had at the old place. And today, Mom and Hannah (three years older than I) and Catherine (one year older) were getting the needed stuff.

Since we were new to the town, Mom had with us a native guide who knew where all the stores were, Lynn Wing. By the way, did I mention that Lynn has read every single book in the Western Hemisphere? I'm sure of it. So she had a trait I really admire, reading, and another I couldn't care less about—knowing where to shop.

Why was I along that morning? Pack mule. In the course of an hour, I took two loads out to the car. Now I dragged along behind Catherine, my hands almost full with a third load. I never wanted to see another place that sold curtains and linens.

Actually, it could have been worse. Hannah had to get back to baby-sit, so this was only a morning trip. Some shopping trips last all day.

And then this tiny voice in the deepest recesses of my gut whispered to me, "Psst, Les! Over there! Look!"

A bicycle shop squeezed between a bookstore and still another bed- and-bath place. And in the window of that bike shop sat the world's greatest ever bike. It didn't just sit there leaning on its kickstand. I tell you, it posed. It wiggled its eyebrows (if it had any). It beckoned. I stopped cold and stared at it, enchanted.

Dazzling paint job with reflecting pinstripes on a deep, luscious, metallic-fleck electric blue. Off-road whitewalls with knobby tread. Built-in sideview mirrors. Bullet headlamp and multi-flashing taillight. Advanced racing gear system on a derailleur. Caliper brakes. I could go on and on. It was blessed with every neat feature known to cycling man. Or cycling woman.

I was still standing there drooling (not for real—that's a figure of speech) when my bossy sister Hannah came harumphing up to me, grabbed me by an arm, and started chewing on me about keeping up.

I suddenly cried, "Whoa!"

Hannah scowled. "Now what?"

"You have all this extra energy, and you're not out of breath from carrying stuff, or you wouldn't have the wind to jump on me like this. Here. You carry them." I dropped the bags of purchases at her feet. "I'll be in the bike shop. Call me when you need me."

"*Leslie Johns Walker!*" When she uses every name I own, I know she's mad. But she couldn't leave the packages lying there in order to chase me, so I made good my escape.

Except for the piped-in music all malls put on their sound systems, the bike shop sat silently. At peace with the universe. From somewhere up in the dark rafters, a spotlight shone down upon *it*. The bike. My bike.

The info tag dangling from the handlebar announced to me that this was not just the Gormann Roadmaster but the Gormann *Super* Roadmaster. The gears ran all the way from sub-granny for cruising up vertical surfaces to ultra-cheetah for outrunning bullet trains. I pictured myself on this bicycle serving as the pace car for the Indy 500.

Beside me, a sales guy appeared out of thin air. He wore those biking clothes that look like they're made from neon-colored inner tubes. When he grinned, the braces on his teeth sparkled. "Cool, huh?"

"Yeah." I tried to sound grown-up like a person buying a car. "What's standard on it?"

"Everything you see. This one's loaded."

I noticed one of those theft-proof U-shaped

locks mounted in its holder on the frame. "Including the lock?"

He nodded. "Everything. Patch kit, water bottle. We even throw in our standard helmet because we believe every cyclist in the world should wear one."

The price tag fluttered from the other handlebar. I turned it around and looked at it. The figure was so large it should have pulled the bike over on itself.

"When's your birthday?" the wily salesman asked.

"Not near soon enough."

Out on the mall on the other side of the show window, here came Mom and Lynn. Behind her, Catherine and Hannah struggled valiantly with bags of stuff. Does a lad's heart good to see them work like that.

Mom entered and scowled, but she seemed more amused than angry. "So you got sidetracked."

"Into the only store in this mall worth going into. Besides the food court, of course." I nodded toward the beautiful bike.

"You already have a good bike."

"Mom, this isn't a bike. It's a cruising machine. A statement to the world. A brilliant engineering masterpiece. A work of art."

Lynn looked at me and then raised one eyebrow. I don't know how she does that. The corner of her mouth tipped up, giving her a yeah-sure- you-betcha leer.

Mom wasn't impressed, either. She snorted.

"We're ready to go. Pry yourself loose." She walked out, which means I walked out. She's never left me behind yet, but there's always a first time.

Mad as a shampooed cat, Hannah thrust her load of bags at me. I took one of them, scooped up a couple of Catherine's, and trotted after Mom.

Mom didn't say anything more about the bike, not even when we got home. Probably she forgot about it. But my fate was sealed. I was in love with that electric-blue Gormann Super Roadmaster.

3

Less than an hour after that shopping trek, Lynn and I met the others as per schedule at Sugar Creek County Park. This was a business meeting. And we always ate our way through business meetings. I brought the bologna sandwiches, Mike brought tortilla chips and dip, Lynn brought cookies, Tiny brought potato chips and Kool-Aid, and Bits brought apples. Two kinds of chips! Now, there's a feast!

We ate lunch in a quiet glade off a side trail, right on the bank of the creek. I suppose the little path down to this spot was originally made by fishermen, but no one had fished there for some time. Except for us, no one seemed to use it anymore.

A dragonfly with dazzling gold glints in its wings zipped in close. Its egg-sized eyes checked us out. Then, I guess, it decided it didn't want any bologna sandwich and zipped away to go catch something tastier—a mosquito, maybe.

High overhead, a blue jay coasted in and started squawking complaints at us. Since we weren't doing anything to complain about, Bits took its grousing as begging and tossed out a potato chip. It did not come to get it.

"What's that?" Lynn waved toward a little

gray bird in the bushes just across the creek. The back of its head was pointed like a blue jay's crest, but its soft gray color looked nothing like the jay's gaudy blue and white.

"Tufted titmouse." Tiny didn't even turn to look at the titmouse. He recognized its raspy cheep while he worked on his sandwich and chips. He knew all the birds, and he almost always carried binoculars around his neck.

I spent most of the lunch enlightening them about the Gormann Super Roadmaster.

Tiny sneered, "It can't be that great."

And I replied, "It's even greater than that. My humble words don't begin to describe its magnificence."

Bits made a realistic choking gesture, but Lynn came to my rescue. "It really is a beautiful bike, Tiny. It looks like a fairly good value for the money."

Fairly good, did she say!

Mike hopped to his feet. "OK, so we gotta see this monster. Then we make up our own minds."

"Good idea!" I stood up and brushed tortilla chip crumbs off my T-shirt. I led the way then out to our ordinary (I could even say *shabby*) bikes with their dull, listless paint jobs. And not a single, solitary pinstripe on the lot.

Besides, at that accident scene, someone had stepped on Tiny's bike, bending the wheel and loosening some spokes. His handlebars were wapper-jawed, too. He was an accident victim, and he wasn't even in the wreck. He had it straightened enough that it worked, mostly, but it sure wasn't pretty.

Mike's bike, though, was especially bad. His frame was rusting out, particularly at the welds. You couldn't even see what color it used to be. Silver duct tape criss-crossed his saddle. I don't think it ever had fenders. It didn't have lights, either; but then, he wasn't allowed out after dark anyway, so he didn't need them.

We rode back streets over to the Brookstone Mall. This morning as I was toting bags behind my mom and sisters, little did I imagine I'd be back in this place again, not only so soon but also voluntarily.

We couldn't find any bike rack. Apparently you were only supposed to drive to the mall. So we chained up our bikes around a light pole. I led my doubting friends directly to the bike shop, carefully avoiding the bed-and-bath on one side and ignoring the bookstore on the other. Mike spotted the Super Roadmaster through the window and blurted a string of Spanish. Tiny entered the shop and approached it almost reverently.

Bits stood there studying it a moment. "So?" She shrugged. "It's a bike."

I couldn't believe she didn't fall in love instantly. "Yeah, sure, and a Cadillac convertible is just another family car."

Mike cooed, "I see me riding this down the street and everybody sees it, they cheer and clap."

Tiny rumbled, "I see going up hills without

having to stand up on the pedals." His voice was deep for his age. "And the spokes are straight."

Lynn nodded. "It is a beautiful color. And it doesn't look like a couple pipes welded together, like mountain bikes do."

"The lock comes with it, huh?" Even the eternal grouch Bits seemed to be getting into it.

And then I got a brainstorm best called a brain-hurricane. "You know, with a little work maybe we could each get one. Matching bikes for the new Sugar Creek Gang!"

"All the extra stuff." Bits grinned. "Front fork shocks and everything. We could jump curbs this high!"

"Yeah. We could go anywhere," Tiny agreed. "Anywhere at all."

"In style!" Mike always got enthusiastic about things, but this time he was bouncing up and down inside his skin. "We could even do traffic stops with it!" Did I mention Mike yearned to be a police officer? He'll be a good one, too.

Lynn looked thoughtful. "I have a college fund started, but I'm not allowed to touch it. So my real savings are pretty small. I'd need a lot more."

"Me too," Bits said. "Right now I could afford the front wheel and maybe the brakes."

"I have cash enough for the brake pads." Tiny looked forlorn. You can get new brake pads for less than two bucks.

"I can buy it if I rob a bank," Mike moaned, "but then I won't be able to be a cop. They don't hire felons."

See? Didn't I tell you he'd be a good officer? He already knew words like *felon*.

In the end we all agreed that my idea was great. But obviously, it was going to need work.

4

To hear Catherine and Hannah talk, that grueling, consuming morning of shopping absolutely wore them out. They couldn't lift a finger. Or turn a page. But somewhere, somehow they found the energy to go someplace with Mom that evening. It was to some female kind of thing; I don't know what exactly. That left Dad and me at home.

Dad had to go to the library. Usually, when I go to the library, I ride my bike. But this evening, since Dad was driving, sure I'd go along. Why pedal an ordinary, everyday bike when you can ride in a car? Of course, were that bike a Super Roadmaster, the picture would be very different.

As Dad was locking the door behind us, who should turn up on the porch but Bits. Did I mention she lives right across the street from us?

Grumpy as usual, she pasted a phony smile on her face. "Hi. You leaving?"

"Hi. Library. Wanna come along?"

"How long will you be gone?"

I shrugged.

Dad said, "A couple hours, probably. You're welcome to join us. Let your father know."

The expression on her face said, *Well, this*

sure isn't the way I planned to spend the evening, but her lips said, "OK. Be right back."

She wasn't any happier at the library than she was on our porch. She poked at the keyboard of a computer terminal, but she didn't really look up anything. She thumbed through some computer magazines in Current Periodicals. She watched over my shoulder as I scanned the New Mysteries shelf, but she didn't reach for anything. She sort of tagged along behind me, close but not quite bumping into me.

I found an old Martin and Osa Johnson African adventure book. Lately, I had been "exploring career options," as Dad put it. What better career than African explorer? I wasn't going to let a little detail like the fact that Africa's already been explored slow me down. And an explorer's life wasn't at all like Bits's goofy computer game. I knew that much.

I also found a video on how to tie nautical knots. You never know when you'll need a nautical knot, right?

Dad made some copies and checked out a couple of books on his card. Bits didn't get anything. She just sort of moped her way out the door behind us and flopped into the backseat of our car. Why did she bother going?

I lowered my passenger-side window, propped an elbow on it, and let the near-dark breeze slather all over me. I pictured myself cruising this street on a Super Roadmaster, the wind in my face just like this. The places I'd go. The things I'd do, if only—

"Stop the car, Dad!" It burst out of me so suddenly it startled even me. In fact, I didn't realize for a moment why I'd said it. "Stop the car!"

"What?" He pulled to the curb. "What's wrong?"

"Smell that? Smoke!"

"Someone's burning trash, or charcoal, or hamburgers on their grill." He started to pull away, but I already had my seat belt popped and the door open.

"No. It's wood smoke. I'm sure."

"Les . . ." Then he must have smelled it, too, because he killed the engine and got out.

Bits pushed in close beside me. "How do you know it's wood smoke?"

"'Cause that's what it smells like." I stood on the sidewalk, turning this way and that, trying to figure out where it might be coming from. Daniel Boone would have tossed a pinch of dust in the air to learn exactly which way the breeze was blowing, then walked right up to the fire.

I'm not Daniel Boone, and besides, there wasn't any dust for half a mile. But the breeze was obviously channeling down an alley here between buildings. So the fire, whatever was burning, would probably be back that alley.

Bits grabbed my arm. "Come on, Les! It's somebody burning leaves. Don't go back an alley when it's almost dark."

I yanked free and headed up the alley with Dad and Bits right behind. "Burning what leaves? It's early summer. You know all the ins and outs around here. Where does the alley go?"

"It cuts across to Bridge Avenue." A few feet farther, she pointed to a big, boxy building. It was greenish in the sallow streetlight. "Up ahead there. Don't you recognize it?"

"That? It's a church. There's a light on inside it, see? It's lighting up a stained glass window." The smoke odor was distinctive now. Definitely wood, like a campfire smells. But this was town. What was burning?

I jogged ahead a few feet farther, and stopped. "Hey! That's *our* church! Now I know where we are. Eight hundred block of Bridge Avenue."

"Bingo." Bits sounded just plain snide.

I recognized the back. The church and its separate classroom annex were wood frame and painted white. So was the maintenance shed beside the church's back door. The memorial garden beside the annex was closed in by a low brick wall with trees and bushes. I recognized our church's parking lot too, with its iron street lamps and round globes. They made normal white light instead of the sickly yellow or green.

Dad moved on ahead. Suddenly he blurted something and snatched his cell phone out of its hip holster. He beeped in three numbers.

Not until he dialed three numbers did I realize what was really happening. Three numbers would be 9-1-1. Emergency. He'd spotted the fire. And now so had Bits and I. Because that dull yellow light behind the stained glass window flickered!

"Oh no!" Bits wailed. "What if the church cat's in there! And the gold candlesticks my grandfather gave them! We have to rescue them!" She darted forward, swift as a greyhound. "We can break a window and get in!"

Dad grabbed her as she whipped past him, before I could even get my feet moving. "No, Bits! You never ever enter a burning building!"

"Yes, but—"

"Never!" Then he went back to talking on the phone to the dispatcher, who obviously was asking him questions.

"I can't just stand here!" Bits howled.

"Neither can I!" I ran to an iron gate in the brick wall. "All the fire extinguishers are locked inside, but there's a garden hose out here in the garden." Now I could see the orange flicker in the plain-glass downstairs window nearest the shed.

"What are we going to squirt it at?"

"I don't know!"

The parking lot lamps cast enough light to find the hose by. I knew pretty much where the faucet was, near the hall door of the annex. With Dad hovering close by, Bits and I got the hose connected. Away off, sirens whined.

Crash! Roar! That plain-glass window exploded outward. A gush of smoke boiled out. The paint on the maintenance shed blistered almost instantly.

There was our target. That shed held the lawn mowers and trimmers—stuff with gas engines. It probably also held gas cans and other things that burn or even blow up. I knew that was where they stored the propane gas grills for youth group cookouts. It was locked, so we couldn't just run in and grab them.

We turned the hose on the shed to cool it down so it wouldn't catch. The shed wall nearest the window hissed and crackled when the water hit it. Gray steam billowed up. The shed smoldered, but it didn't ignite.

The sirens wailed louder, louder, louder!

Dad hurried out front to direct the firefighters. While Bits continued to wash the shed down, I found a second hose. I was looking for another faucet when the fire truck came lumbering back the alley, frantically splashing red, white, and blue lights on the buildings all around.

Bits and Dad and I backed off, of course. We moved away a safe distance and watched. A firefighter on top of the tanker truck started spraying water onto the shed and in the window. Others had already laid hose, faster than you can imagine, from the hydrant out front.

The firefighters who broke the door down and entered the church wore gruesome masks and air tanks. They breathed from the air supply they took with them—not the fatal fumes inside the building. As they stepped inside, they sprayed the fire ahead of them with big sweeping swishes from their hose. Crowded together in a cluster, they disappeared instantly into the black ink of smoke.

I remembered then that, in a building fire, it's almost never the flames that get you. It's the smoke and poisonous gases you breathe while you're trying to get out. That's why you always stay down as low as you can, because most of the smoke and poison gases rise. If Bits had smashed her way in there, she would have keeled over dead in seconds.

The firefighters ran around—they scurried —but you could tell there was nothing purposeless or confused about what they did. Everything flowed. They used amazing equipment —from the truck itself, massive and dazzling, to their heavy outfits with vivid reflector stripes.

Being an African explorer is very nice, I'm sure, and fun and exciting. But for fun and excitement, you couldn't do much better than the scene before us just now. I could save lives and property and make a real difference, and I wouldn't even have to leave town.

I'd been wondering a lot about what I might do when I grew up. Firefighter was looking mighty good.

5

You've heard the saying "It's not what you know, it's who you know." Which, incidentally, is not correct English, Mom tells me. The correct word is *whom,* not *who.* I have no idea why, but since Mom is an English teacher, I'll bet I find out sometime. Anyway, it turned out that Bits and I sure knew the right people.

Bits's dad, Jim Ware, is a sergeant on the police force. My dad, Bill Walker, is a lawyer. Jim Ware helps the pastor out with jail ministries and stuff. Dad represents the church when they need legal advice—a *pro bono* thing, which means for free. Dad and Bits's dad claim they're the church's official pig and shark. (Hey, those are their words, not mine. They laugh when they say it.)

Anyway, Sergeant Ware and Dad wangled it so that they could tag along when the fire marshal investigated the church fire.

And here's the great part: Bits and I got to go along, too! So there stood the four of us at eight in the morning, hanging around in the church parking lot, waiting for the fire marshal to arrive.

From the front, the church didn't look a bit different. But out back here was a hideous mess. The whole rear side of the building was cordoned off with yellow plastic ribbon-tape: POLICE LINE DO NOT CROSS. The back of the church was hacked with ax marks. The broken door gaped open. Broken windows stared sightless. Chopped pieces of charred wood and roofing shingles and chunks of attic insulation lay all over. Bushes were trampled and broken. The poor little old shed huddled against the church wall, scorched and blistered, and some of its wood had warped.

And the stink! Wet wood smells bad. Soak it with a fire hose, and it smells much, much worse. Add to that the stench of all the other things that had burned or melted.

A white sedan pulled up, but it wasn't the fire marshal. The lieutenant who'd directed the firefighters last night parked, got out, and crossed to us.

As he greeted Dad and the sergeant, we learned his name was Grover. Then he smiled at Bits and me. "We're thinking of doing a video for fire prevention week. Show it in the schools this October. We'd like you two to be in it. You made all the right moves last night. You're heroes."

Heroes? *Heroes?*

"And because of that," the lieutenant continued, "I made a special deal with the fire marshal to let you come along today at your dads' request." The smile faded. "The fire marshal never lets little kids go along on something like this. I need you both to promise you'll do what you're asked and stay out of the way."

Bits and I couldn't promise fast enough, believe me!

And then the fire marshal arrived in a white car pretty much like Lieutenant Grover's. The man, Mr. Meyers, looked kind of like Santa Claus without the beard—short and round and pleasant. He was almost bald. Not quite.

He looked Bits and me over. "So you two were gonna put our fire out, eh?" He bobbed his head, a Santa-like gesture. "I want you both to know I don't do this as a rule—let you go along, I mean."

Lieutenant Grover asked, "Fred coming?"

"Half an hour or so." Mr. Meyers just stood there studying the back of the church. I could see where his eyes were looking. He started at the top, staring at the eaves. Then the windows. He stepped back a few feet to be able to see to the roof. Then he walked over and examined the shed briefly.

I blurted out, "Can you explain what you're looking at? Looking for, I mean."

He glanced at me and half smiled. "Sure. If a fire is arson, the arsonist has to break into the building in some way—at least get his match and accelerant inside. What do you see about those two windows? He pointed to what was left of the plain-glass windows by the shed.

"They're broken. We saw that nearest one blow out last night, but we didn't see the other one go."

Santa nodded. "Good. But let's say you didn't

see that near one go. How would you know it broke in the fire?"

Bits chimed in, "Because the glass is outside! If someone broke it to get in, the glass would be inside on the floor."

I probably would have thought of that.

Mr. Meyers nodded. "Exactly! And where's the broken glass from that other window?"

"Inside. So—"

"Right." He nodded again. In fact, it was a sort of continuous bobbing nod. "Now why do I know that the firefighters broke it—not an arsonist—in order to throw water on the fire?"

That was a tough one. I studied it and could think of nothing. Neither could Bits.

Lieutenant Grover grinned. "I'll give you a hint. Captain Meyers here read my report this morning."

Now I got it. "You write that stuff down in your report after the fire."

"Right. So we don't think there's an arsonist when there wasn't."

Captain Meyers started for the open door. "You kids stay close to your dads. Don't walk anywhere an adult hasn't been first. The floor might be weakened, and you can't tell that it's dangerous." From a clip on his belt, Captain Meyers yanked out the hugest flashlight I ever saw. It put out a beacon bright enough to guide airplanes in.

He stepped inside from sun to gloom. Dad followed and moved in beside him. I pressed close to Dad.

Was it scary? Yeah! Really dark. The power was out, of course. The firefighters had thrown the switch first thing when they arrived, Dad said last night, to prevent shorts and electrical fires. So it was *really* dark inside. But the walls and ceiling were black from flames and smoke, which made it darker than dark.

Did I say it smelled outside? Man, that was nothing compared to inside here. You could hardly breathe.

The air hung very heavy, still warm and wet from the fire hoses' water. The leftover puddles would probably have made the tile floor slippery, but too much debris littered it. You couldn't walk anywhere without crunching charred wood or fabric or broken glass or strange, unidentifiable trash.

When you read about a fire in the paper or see some TV reporter standing and talking in front of a building, you can't possibly imagine what it's really like inside. It's smellier and more horrible than TV can show.

Sergeant Ware asked all kinds of technical questions I didn't understand. Since I'd never been in the back of the church before, I didn't know what it used to be like. So I couldn't compare. Bits, though, had been in here. She looked near tears.

Captain Meyers traced the wiring, looking for wires that sort of explode as they melt. Apparently you can tell from how it looks whether a wire shorted out, indicating an electrical cause, but he couldn't find an example to show us.

"See the alligator charring?" He pointed with his flashlight to a place on the wall. The fire had turned the surface of a wooden beam into a grid of black rectangles separated by deep grooves.

I moved in closer to see better. "That's how campfire wood looks sometimes."

"Only the hottest fires can char wood in that pattern. It burned hot in here for a pretty long time."

Bits asked, "So here is where the fire started?"

"Comparing the other areas of damage, almost certainly."

"Fred's here!" Lieutenant Grover called.

Know who Fred was? A dog! A big, happy, yellow Labrador retriever. His handler, a uniformed fire department officer, gave him a treat and sent him off. You can't beat a lab for sheer enthusiasm. Happy as a mudlark in a swamp, Fred trotted all over the litter-strewn floor, poking his nose here, sniffing there.

Now dogs have much better sniffers than people do. Hundreds of times better, in fact. So to me, that meant the stench in that building was hundreds of times worse for Fred than for me. But he sure didn't seem to notice it.

Suddenly he sat down, his tail wagging wildly.

"Show me!" said his handler.

He poked his nose around a burned table and sat down again, ready for a treat. His tail flailed. The handler gave him some goody and sent him off to look for more.

Bits frowned. "What did he just find?"

Her dad looked grim. "The dog is trained to locate accelerants."

"What's that?"

"Oil or gasoline—something that gets a fire going quickly."

Arson.

6

Mom has this notion that dinner is supposed to be family time. Nobody is allowed to bring a book or anything else to the table. We have to be polite, using *please* and *thank you*. We can't badger sisters (or brothers). And we even have to use the right silverware correctly.

I know what you're thinking, and you're right. Eleven-year-old boys don't fit into that scene any better than they fit into shopping. But like going shopping, I didn't have a choice. That was the way it was. Mom says someday I'm going to want to impress a girl (she actually said that!) or a boss (OK, maybe a boss) or someone else important to me. And I'll need to know how to eat politely.

Hannah and Catherine take to that kind of thing naturally. I have to work at it.

So anyway, here we were around the table. Hannah talked about her almost-every-day baby-sitting job and how spoiled and bossy the two children were. Catherine described a new friend up the street whose mother manages a toy store and lets her test new toys.

Bits knocked on the door. When I answered it and told her we were eating, she said her computer was on the fritz and asked if she

35

could use mine. We said, "Sure," and she disappeared into the back of the house with a joystick sticking out of her jeans pocket. I went back to dinner.

Mom said that tomorrow she was going to the school district office to interview. She was looking for a teaching job here. Dad, of course, already had a job; that's why we moved here from Seattle.

The fire marshal thing had been that morning. But Dad didn't say anything about the church fire, and I wasn't allowed to say anything either. He drummed it into us kids years ago that you never ever, *ever, EVER* talk about a case.

Then I casually asked Hannah how much money baby-sitting brings in.

She looked at me in that superior way of hers. "You're too young to baby-sit."

"Thanks for the answer to 'Why can't I baby-sit?' But the question was, 'How much you gonna rake in?'"

Dad laughed out loud.

Mom smiled. "A born lawyer, Bill. Scary." The smile fled. "Don't tell me you're thinking about that bike."

"OK. I won't tell you. I don't have to, right? You already guessed."

"What bike?" Dad asked.

Talk about a perfect opportunity! So I described it to him. Just to emphasize what a splendid bike it was, I also described Mike and Tiny's reaction when they first saw it. I neglected to mention Bits's put-down (*So? It's a bike.*) You can get too much detail into a presentation.

It was Hannah's week to help with dishes, so I didn't have to waste time in the kitchen. I followed Dad out to his den and settled on the sofa beside him as he reached for the TV remote.

Silence, except for the TV.

Dad muted the TV and made the silence complete. Finally he asked, very offhandedly, "So you're planning a career as a professional baby-sitter."

"Nah. I'll let Hannah do that. Actually, I was kind of thinking of being a firefighter, until we got to watch the fire marshal work this morning. Now I'm thinking maybe that's what I'd like to do. Be a fire marshal. Or a dog handler."

Dad managed to run through the whole channel selection in less than a minute, but there's only eight of them; we don't get cable. "I'm glad you got to go along."

"Yeah, so am I. That was so great."

More silence.

Then Dad commented as he settled on the public TV channel, "Wasn't too long ago that you said you wanted to be a mystery writer. Because you like to solve mysteries."

"I read somewhere that lots of writers have other jobs besides writing. I could do both."

Long, thick silence.

"I like to solve mysteries, too." Dad cranked the TV volume up, didn't seem too interested in the natural history of the Himalayan tahr, and turned the volume back down. "For instance, there's Bits in the back of the house there, playing computer games on your machine, but here you sit out here. Why you're not back there with her is a mystery."

"How do you know she's playing games?"

"I saw the joystick. So did you. Analyzing this mystery, I deduct that you are going to approach me about some creative financing for that bike you covet. How much is it?"

What could I do? He was onto me. When I told him the price, all he said was, "You already have a bike."

"Yeah, but this is the difference between owning a used Toyota and a new Lear jet."

He chuckled, but it faded too fast. Altogether serious, he said, "If you want a more expensive bike, Les, you'll have to buy it yourself."

"Yes, but . . ." But what? I'm getting pretty good at reading his tone of voice—Mom's too—and I knew we had just reached the end of the discussion. Sometimes Dad can be— what do you call it?—cajoled. Convinced otherwise. Conned into saying *yes*. Not this time.

The nature show got bored with tahrs and started talking about takins instead—weird goatlike antelopes (pronounced tah-*keen,* in case you ever want to work it into a conversation). I watched a few minutes and wandered back to see how Bits was doing.

She was losing. You could tell from the look

on her face, more sour than usual. And that's *sour*. She didn't even look up when I walked in.

I watched over her shoulder a few minutes. Play roared along hot and heavy, and she was doing OK. But then a big pit yawned open, and her game figure fell into it. Blackout.

"I can never get past level eleven!"

"I didn't know that game had eleven levels. How do you get through the brick wall in level five?"

"That's a no-brainer. Just tunnel. The wall in seven is the one you have to worry about. You can't tell what's on the other side, and it's one of three monsters." She started level eleven again.

I flopped down on the rug beside her, tired of watching her game figure jump around. "Do you have all these games memorized?"

"Some of them. Hey, do you have Galactic War Three on this machine? I couldn't find it."

"I don't have Galactic War One. When did they come out with Three?"

"Week ago. I'm surprised you don't have it."

"I'm surprised you spend so much of your life playing computer games."

She glared, not at me but at the monitor. I could tell it was meant for me, though. "You sound like my dad, so cut it out."

And then my keen mystery-reading-trained brain clicked. "He kicked you out of your house, right? He thinks you play computer games too much, and he told you to go do something else awhile. In fact, I bet that when we were going to the library yesterday, he'd just chased you away from your computer then too."

She looked furious, even though she didn't slow down play. I had nailed the head right on the hit.

So I changed the subject. "Did you talk to your dad about the bike?"

Wrong subject. Now she *really* looked mad! "He says I have enough bikes."

"Mm. Yeah, my dad says about the same thing." I could feel my idea— matched bikes for the whole gang—going nowhere fast.

Bits didn't pause a second as she maneuvered her game figure through a forest full of sharp-toothed creatures who waited behind trees. "So does Lynn's. What did you say to her, anyway? Now she's all hot to buy one of those things. She's thinking up fund-raisers and everything."

"She is?" If anyone could come up with a practical, effective way to make money, it would be Lynn. Lynn or Tiny.

I figured maybe I ought to go talk to Lynn. Better, I would e-mail around to the gang to meet at the park.

That is, if I could wrest my computer away from Miss Game-Player long enough to send the message.

7

Now here's something to be when you grow up: You own this company that goes in and cleans up extra-messy messes. They don't do regular cleaning. They only tackle special jobs. I watched a company like that do its work the next morning at the church.

The fire had done terrible things to the back rooms of the church. But so had the water. When the firemen sprayed their hoses, everything got drenched—carpets, draperies, books and papers, you name it. Water from the burning area poured out into the sanctuary and soaked that carpeting also. Smoke darkened the auditorium walls and ceilings and clouded the windows. The whole church stank, every room. Even the choir robes and stuff smelled like smoke.

Clean Machine to the rescue! That was the name of the company. They pulled up to go to work just as the church board was beginning a business meeting. As the church's new legal counsel, Dad was invited to sit in on the meeting, and he'd let me come along to the church. Bits's dad is a board member, and he brought Bits along—against her will, I might add, so she pouted and took her bad humor out on me. Boy, was she cranky!

So here came four women in a three-quarter-ton truck. They parked by the back door and immediately started unloading some major equipment. They had vacuum cleaners big as a kitchen table. They had fans you could propel an airplane with. They had tubs and buckets and cans full of stuff. They gave the pastor a cheery greeting and got right to work. And it was work that looked kind of like fun.

They started in the sanctuary. Their vacuum cleaners sucked up the water as well as soot and crud. They set their enormous fans up in the doors to air out the vast room.

This really looked interesting. I figured out which woman was in charge; she worked as hard as anyone else, but directed things. I went over and asked her if I could help.

She smiled. "Sorry. I'd hire you in a minute, but you're under age. Child labor laws." She was probably Mom's age, but her eyes crinkled up so much when she smiled that she looked old.

"OK, you can't pay me, but is there something I can do?" And then I added, "It's my church," although we were not members yet.

She hesitated a moment. "Sure." She raised her voice. "Marlee? This guy wants to help. Let him sprinkle the dust." She pointed. "Go see the blonde over there."

I crossed the sanctuary to Marlee.

Marlee, the blonde, looked barely out of high school. I liked her happy smile. "Here." She handed me a bucketful of powder and a sifter sort of thing. "This powder kills mold and mildew in damp carpeting. After we've gotten as much water out as we can, we dust the carpet with this. Like this, see?" She dipped the sifter thing into the powder and flicked it around like a fairy godmother trying to toss sparkles on everything in sight.

So for the next half hour, while Dad met with the board and who knows where Bits wandered off to, I sprinkled mildew preventer on the church's carpeting. It was a lot more fun than pouting.

"Coffee break!" the boss announced.

Marlee whistled to me across the sanctuary and dipped her head. "Come on and take a break!"

Sure! I wasn't about to tell them I don't drink coffee.

Out back in the parking lot, they broke open a cooler of soft drinks. I picked a cola out of the ice and sat on the ground beside the tailgate.

I asked Marlee, "Do you always get these really terrible messes to clean up?"

"This isn't bad."

"Maybe not in the sanctuary. But the other room—"

"That's not bad either. Bad is when you're cleaning up after a murder."

"A mur—" Wow. When I thought about challenging special jobs, I'd never thought of something like that.

"Ever stop to consider?" Marlee asked.

43

"After a murder, someone has to clean up the mess, right? Blood and everything, all over. You can't imagine what a mess. A hundred times worse than what they show in movies. And the stink—they can't show that in the movies, but believe me, it's there. So we come in and clean up the apartment or store or whatever so it looks like nothing ever happened. Sometimes it's easiest to just recarpet and repaint."

I thought about that awhile. Now there's a career you don't consider every day—a very useful one for the innocent victims. I'm made for it, too. A natural. Messes don't bother me. In fact, when Mom wants me to clean up my room, which is very frequently, she claims I live in the world's worst mess.

Of course, Mom had not seen the inside of the church here.

We worked until lunch, pushing a broom in the back room, bagging all that debris. Then Dad and Sergeant Ware came out of the meeting, and Bits tagged along behind them. I said good-bye, and as I left, the boss tucked a bill into my hand.

I protested, "I just enjoyed working. Thank you for letting me. I wasn't expecting pay. Really. Besides, you aren't supposed to pay me."

"You're a good worker, and you were a real help. That's not pay. That's a thank you."

I wasn't sure what the correct thing to do was, so I said again, "I enjoyed it. Thank you very much," stuffed the bill in my pocket without looking at it, and ran to catch up with Dad and Bits and her father.

We went to the Extraburger for lunch, one of those places with the menu in lights over the french fries. You know: gourmet fast food. Bits and I sat at one table for two, and Dad and her dad sat across the aisle.

I took a peek at the thank-you bill the cleaning lady had handed me. It was a twenty! I stuffed it back in my pocket. If Dad saw it, he might get second thoughts about buying my lunch for me.

Sergeant Ware paused after a bite of very drippy—and therefore delicious—burger. He frowned. "The church's budget is already committed to ministries and missions. You heard them discuss it, Bill. I don't see how we can afford the rebuilding that the insurance won't cover. We're down to skin and bones now."

Dad nodded. "Your financial officer shouldn't have gone with less insurance than you needed."

"It wasn't his fault. We didn't have the money for the big policy."

Dad asked, "Did you come up with any leads on the cause of the fire?"

"We put some foot soldiers on the trail around the area. A neighbor across the street from the church saw a kid on a bike, looking suspicious. The boy stopped in front of the church and hung around in the shadows a few minutes. Then he pedaled away fast. No way at this point to get a make on him."

I looked at Bits. She knew police jargon. "Foot soldiers?"

"Police officers walking from door to door asking questions."

"And 'getting a make' is identifying, right?" I'd read enough mysteries to know that much.

She nodded.

Sergeant Ware gestured. "In fact, you might keep an eye out. The church is in our neighborhood, and the kid might live near here. Small, dark—the witness thinks Hispanic —on a beat-up bike. Green shirt, jeans."

Bits mumbled, "That could be anybody."

I muttered, "It could be Mike."

Then her dad added, "The only odd thing—she remembered a metal bike seat."

Metal bike seat? I never heard of anybody with a metal bike seat.

But our friend and fellow Sugar Creeker little Mike Alvarado held his bike seat together with lots of silver duct tape.

8

Tall Sugar Creeker Tiny Wilson had the world's greatest volunteer job. About five miles outside town was an old chicken farm. Someone had converted it into a kind of hospital —a shelter—for taking care of wild animals that were hurt. When you found an injured rabbit, for instance, or a nest of baby birds that fell out of a tree, you brought them to this place and someone could help them. One of the someones was Tiny.

Mike Alvarado lived only a couple of houses away from Tiny. In fact, Mike often went along with Tiny to help at the animal rescue shelter. So that afternoon, I rode my bike out there.

Bits insisted she wanted to stay home, and I know it was so she could lose more game figures in open pits. She didn't even ask me why I was going. I was going because that business about a metal bike seat bothered me so much.

I already mentioned that we aren't ever allowed to talk about a case, so I could not let out a peep to Tiny or Mike about what I heard from Bits's dad. I could not tell them anything about a suspect with a beat-up bike. Not about anything at all. That was all secret information.

So how could I bring up the subject? I was

pedaling back the gravel lane to the shelter when I figured out how to do it.

I passed a little house and garage and headed for the first of three long sheds with no windows in them. Rickety pens and corrals stood around everywhere, a big hodgepodge of chicken wire and wooden frames. Most of the homemade pens were a couple feet off the ground, perched on two-by-four legs.

There was no bike rack at the shelter, but you never bothered to chain up your bike there anyway. No need to. I just dumped mine on the grass beside Tiny's. He had lost a couple of his spokes, I noticed. I walked in the front door of the nearest shed.

This long, large reception room was equipped to give an animal first aid. You could weigh the animal ("So you know how big a medicine dose to give it," Tiny once explained) and put it in a correct-size cage. There were all kinds of tools to hold an animal still, a couple of operating tables, and cabinets full of medicine bottles. What a great place to work!

Tiny stood near the front door at a big trash can full of birdseed, filling cups with a scoop. At the other side of the room, Mike was loading a dishwasher with custard cups. They wore the shelter's uniform, you might call it— blue jeans and a green T-shirt with the shelter's name on front and back. They hello-ed me, and I hello-ed them.

I crossed the room to Mike. "I didn't think you were here. I didn't see your bike out front."

"I rode out on Tiny's handlebars. My bike's busted, and I mean busted. A weld rusted through, and the whole frame broke apart when I hit a pothole. Dad is gonna try to weld it, but he doesn't think he can."

"That's too bad." And I thought, *Boy, if any-one needs a new bike, here he is.* I waved a hand toward the dishwasher. "You guys used to wash cups by hand. When did you get the machine?"

Mike grinned. "Last week. Donation. The door latch is busted, but the washer washes just fine." He closed the door and flicked the switch. The dishwasher started its rhythmic *shiggeda, shiggeda, shiggeda.* Mike grabbed up a roll of duct tape, tore off a couple of lengths, and taped the door shut. "So it don't leak." He was sure good at using duct tape. He could even tear it without using his teeth.

Then the two of us went over to Tiny. It's tough to just stand around doing nothing, so I helped. Using scoops, we filled crockery dishes with dog food from another of those big garbage-size cans.

"Hey, you guys," I said. "I'm still thinking about bikes. Either of you ever see an all-metal bike saddle?"

Tiny frowned. "Who'd want one? You wouldn't sit on a steel seat long before you wanna walk. Pain hurts."

"Except I have one. You remember my bike seat, Les. It's silver." Mike cackled. "That's 'cause they was all out of gold ones."

And we all laughed.

Then we loaded the filled dishes into a beat-up old red coaster wagon and spent the next fifteen minutes dragging that wagon all over the property. We fed an amazing bunch of animals. Two cages of half-grown raccoons got the dog food. So did a down-covered nestling vulture. We gave the seed to songbirds, some mice, and three half-grown pheasants. Tiny hand-fed dog food morsels to a hawk with a broken wing. He tossed a head of wilting leaf lettuce into the rabbits' cage. He said he'd give them rabbit pellets tomorrow.

In short, we had a great time. If I were a real detective, like those in the stories I read, I would have asked a couple of sneaky questions so that Mike or Tiny wouldn't know what I was actually trying to find out. I would get the information I needed to figure out the culprit, and they'd never even know they gave it to me.

But I am not a real detective.

I couldn't think of a solitary question. So I never did find out whether Mike's bike really had broken. I mean, what if he merely ditched it, hiding it because he was afraid it had been identified at the church? And that if anyone saw that "metal" bike saddle, they would point a finger at him and shout, "You're the one! Arsonist!"

9

Lynn was the one who called the meeting. Incidentally, that's a major difference between the old Sugar Creek Gang and us. We use e-mail. Lynn and I have our own accounts. Bits and Tiny use their dads', and Mike gets his info from Tiny, since those two live close together.

So Lynn put out the word late that night, and we all got it the first thing next morning. By ten, we were sprawled out in various positions on the bank of Sugar Creek, eating day-old doughnut holes. Yep. Feeding our faces. That means it was another business meeting.

"The topic of discussion is making money for bikes," Lynn opened. "For starters, I suggest we each put aside fifteen percent of everything we get. More if possible. That's allowance, birthday gifts, everything. My father says it will surprise us how fast it adds up."

Bits wailed, "But *Jungle Peril* is coming out with a new version this month! After I get that, I will."

"You're nuts!" OK, so I wasn't very diplomatic. "It's the world's most boring game."

"Well, the new version won't be."

Tiny nodded. "Saving a percent sounds good, Lynn. Any objections, anybody? Except

Bits." He looked from face to face, but all our faces were busy chewing pretty dry doughnut holes.

Mike looked uncomfortable and kind of squirmed around, but then he squirmed all the time.

Tiny called for a vote. "In favor? Opposed? We got four in favor and one abstain. Passed."

The abstention was Mike. He didn't vote. He just sat there.

Tiny continued, "Also, I found this ad in a magazine." He whipped out a torn page. "You call this number, and you can make big money stuffing envelopes. It figures, right? Think of all the junk mail your parents get. Somebody had to put every one of those letters into an envelope and seal it. It's summer. We got time on our hands. We can do that."

We took turns reading the ad.

I started grinning like a loon. "It says, 'Make a hundred to five hundred dollars a day in your spare time at home. No experience needed. We train you.' You know they couldn't say that if it wasn't true. Man, we'll have bikes in no time!"

Lynn frowned. "Actually, it sounds too good. You know how they always say, 'If it sounds too good to be true, it probably is'? Why aren't millions of people jumping in to do this?"

"'Cause they all have jobs and work all day. We don't." I asked, "Tiny? You call the number here yet?"

"Yeah. Nice guy answered. He says, first we

send them ninety-nine dollars for the tools and equipment. Cashier's check. Not a personal check. They can't just give the stuff to us, because people rip them off. Some people would take their equipment and then use it working for someone else."

Bits nodded. "Sounds right. Dad says the world is full of people like that."

"Sure. Your dad's a cop." Mike, the future cop, reached for another doughnut hole. "He sees them all the time."

Tiny went on. "Then you start to work. 'On your kitchen table,' the guy said. 'Five hundred a pop,' and there's no age restrictions. I asked about that. I can even do it at the shelter when there's nothing to do but someone has to keep the place open."

Lynn shook her head. "Do me a favor, please. Right now we would have to borrow at least some of that start-up money. So before we send them the ninety-nine dollars, let's ask our parents to look it over."

"Look." Tiny waved the ad. "It's just a little thing, right? Pick-up work for in-between times. But it's got really great potential."

I was raring to go. "I agree."

Tiny added, "Lynn, I talked to the guy. He's OK. You can trust him."

She crossed her arms. "If you want my cooperation, you have to show it to one of the fathers first. If it's a scam, they're more likely to see it than we would." Her voice softened. "Tiny, it's only one more day."

Bits shrugged. "She's got a point. There're more scams out there than suckers. Dad says even he doesn't recognize them all."

Tiny scowled, angry-looking. Suddenly he stuck the ad in my hand. "Your dad's the lawyer. Ask him. We'll meet here tomorrow afternoon. I'll bring some crackers. Anybody got strawberry jam?"

"I'll bring jam." Lynn smiled. "Thank you, Tiny."

And the soft way she smiled, and her gentle *thank you*, showed you right there how much it pays to be polite. Tiny sweetened up immediately, and I'm sure it was that genuine thank you that turned him.

So I took the ad home with me, all ready to send the money and start raking it in. I didn't know why Lynn felt so suspicious. Tiny had made the phone call, and he passed on the guy. But I promised I would run it past Dad, so I ran it past Dad.

After supper he went out on the front porch swing to read the paper and sip his coffee. I followed him out with the cordless phone and the ad and sat down beside him.

He looked at me. "I don't get to read my paper until after you're in bed, is that right?"

"Actually, you'll be free of pestering in about twenty minutes. Bits and I are going to youth group tonight. Remember, you're the one who said I had to buy my own bike? So the Creekers are going to make lots of money with this ad." I stuck it in his hand. "And we'll all get matching Super Roadmasters." I flashed him a winning smile. Anyway, I hoped it was winning.

He read the ad and nodded. "So what do you need me for?"

"Lynn thinks it's too good to be true. She'd like you to check it out. You know, pass on it."

"I see." He studied it a moment, took the phone, and punched in the number listed.

Now my dad is great at accents. It's kind of like a hobby with him. He can sound German or French, like a Bostonian in a hurry, like a cowboy from Arizona—you name it. And I love it when he shifts into one.

This time he made himself sound like somebody with a third-grade education who can't use English well. "Uh, good evening, sir. I'm calling about this here ad to make money. A hunnerd to five hunnerd, it says." Then he sat listening awhile, saying, "Uh huh," from time to time.

"Izzat so! Yeah." Long pause. "I guess ninety-nine don't seem too bad if'n I can make it back before the first of the month. That's when my rent's due." Another pause. "OK. I guess that's reasonable."

I was dying to hear what the other fellow was saying, but I couldn't quite make it out. Dad sounded as if he was satisfied. Just about the only chore that was left was for us to count all that money we'd be making.

Then Dad said, "Yessir, I got one question. If I put all these mail pieces together and then send them out from here, how do you know that I did it right? You can't see 'em first. For all you know, I just dumped the whole caboodle in the trash and told you I done it. Lied. Know what I mean?"

Dad looked at me, and his eyelids dropped to half mast, sort of like Charlie Chan in those old mystery videos. "Oh. Uh-huh. I see. Then you send me my money, right?"

He listened, "OK, but *then* you send me my money, izzat right? Why not?" He was smiling now, but his voice sounded so sad. "Oh. Uh-huh. I see."

And then for five minutes at least, he kept telling the person on the other end that he wasn't ready to send the money quite yet, but he had to think about it. I could tell the other person was really pushing on him to send that money right away. And my hopes sank lower and lower. Because the more Dad grunted and uh-huhed and argued, the more clearly I could see it was a scam.

No hundreds of dollars.

No bikes.

10

Ever get the feeling that your life would be a lot easier if you'd just keep your big mouth shut? Boy, that happens to me too often to count. It happened in youth group at church that night.

Bits and I were with the younger kids, and Hannah and Catherine went off with the teenagers. We gathered in a big, smoke-smelly classroom with the window wide open. The older kids put on a skit for us, and we sang some songs. So far, it was pretty much like camp.

The leader, Stan McCorkle, was a youngish adult in jeans and a movie-star-style haircut. He asked about new kids, and Bits introduced me. I hate that, everybody staring at you.

Then the leader started talking about the summer activities. He explained how much damage the fire had caused. Even the roof was going to have to be rebuilt, because the fire weakened the rafters. He apologized that some of the programs would have to be cut back because of the budget crunch. Then he said we could vote on which ones to keep and which to dump.

He named off the activities we would choose from: a skating party, an outdoor concert, a chili feed, a book fair, a trip to the zoo, a different outdoor concert, an evening all to ourselves at the YMCA pool, and some other stuff like that.

Next he asked for comments from everybody. So all of them waved their hands in the air for a chance to say nice words about their favorites and try to swing some votes.

After a few minutes of that, Stan (he insisted a couple times over that he was to be called "Stan," *not* "Mr. McCorkle") looked square at me. Me? I didn't have any opinion on this stuff. I didn't even . . .

"Les?" he was saying. "You haven't seen the schedule before. So you can comment on it from a fresh perspective. Does anything in it particularly appeal to you, or turn you off?"

The silence got thick enough to walk on. Everyone looked at me, waiting for me to say something. What could I do? Then he motioned for me to stand up. Now I was *really* the center of attention!

And the craziest notion zipped through my head: How come the people in the Bible could always stand up and say exactly the right stuff—like Paul and Stephen? That's not anything I ever experienced. And just as fast, another thought zipped by: They didn't. It was God speaking through them. But that was different. Way different. I couldn't imagine Him using me.

I stood up. "Well, uh . . ." *Nice start. Bumblemouth.* I stood straighter and raised my voice. Maybe if I didn't sound so scared, I wouldn't

58

feel so scared. "I'm not the one to ask because I've never been to a youth group meeting before, ever. The church I came from in Ballard —that's a neighborhood in Seattle, Washington —it didn't have one."

"Too small?" the leader asked.

"No, we were big. But they had these ideas about what a church should do. Like missions. And helping the needy. And Bible study. Those were some of the big things. Entertaining kids was no item at all. So as soon as you got into, say, second or third grade, you started helping with grown-up projects. Like, the first thing I ever did was help refinish dining room furniture at the church's nursing home."

The words came easier now. I went on. "Everything you listed for us to vote on is really neat and fun. But it's all free-time stuff. Play. Maybe, I'd think, maybe instead of skating and stuff, it would be best this summer to help the church get money to replace stuff it lost in the fire, and help paint and clean up. That kind of stuff. It just seems like a time to work, not play." I shrugged. "Anyway, that's my suggestion." And I sat down again.

Besides being relieved it was over, I felt pretty disgusted with myself. I'd stumbled over words, ran on, and didn't say nearly as much as I wanted to. I remembered saying *stuff* at least three times, maybe more.

And the silence hung just as heavy after I sat down.

Then a tall girl in the corner stood up. "I

think he's right on. This isn't your average summer. This year the church needs our help, and I think we should just put the whole schedule aside until next summer. This summer we should all work and get our church fixed back up."

Stan made a sweeping gesture. "How about the rest of you? How do you feel about this?"

The silence broke. Apparently it was a really popular idea!

A nerdy-looking boy up front asked, "Do you think the church will let us help?"

"That's a good question." Stan was smiling. "There are child labor laws in this state, but I'm sure there are in Les's state too. It obviously didn't stop them. So I'm assuming we can work OK."

"Can we do real grown-up stuff?" another kid asked.

"That's what we're talking about here. Making an important contribution. Not child's play." Stan was now grinning wide enough to insert a ski. "Tell you what. I'll talk to pastor Earnhart about this. And, Les—get me the phone number at your Seattle church, and I'll call your pastor. I'll see how they do it there."

He looked from face to face. "I can't tell you kids how proud of you I am! Your selflessness is magnificent! Just magnificent! And very much like Jesus."

They spent another fifteen minutes talking about fund-raisers. They could do things to make money for the church, regardless of what else they could do.

And me? I just sort of sat there dumbfounded. I mean, I made a suggestion, one suggestion, that I hadn't really thought through. And this group bought it. It may sound like a little thing to you, but it floored me. No arguments, no changes, no yelling at me. They simply accepted it flat out. Can you imagine that?

That never happened to me before, not anywhere.

11

Lunch today on the banks of Sugar Creek was not exactly a feast with porterhouse steak, two kinds of chips, and chocolate ice cream—or whatever your idea of a great feast would be. Lynn brought sandwiches, and they were tofu lunch-spread on whole wheat bread. Nutritious I am sure, but . . . Mike brought one of those two-for-a-dollar cupcake packs. Mom thought we ought to have apples. So did Tiny's mom. We therefore had two each of the same kind of apples (the ones on special at Grocery Mart).

But, as Tiny pointed out, it was food, which a whole lot of people in the world didn't have any of. So we ate it, and he wouldn't let us complain.

"About that envelope-stuffing job. What the guy on the phone didn't make clear to you, Tiny—" I talked between mouthfuls "—is that you don't just stuff envelopes and send them back. You have to send them out to people on a mailing list. You might send your stuffed envelopes to thousands of people, but you only get paid for the people who accept the offer, whatever it is, and send an order in. In other words, if they throw the mailing away, you don't get paid for that one."

"Yes, but—"

"Also, you have to buy the mailing list to send the stuffed envelopes to."

"Yes, but—"

"And Dad says a mailing list is only good for a year or two, because so many people move or get married or die or something. And he doesn't think the company would keep its lists up to date much. Also, you have to have a bulk mailing permit, and they're a hundred and fifty dollars."

"Maybe that's what the ninety-nine is. A special deal."

"No, it's separate. The post office sells the permit, not the company."

Bits made a face. "Well, that kills that."

Lynn looked forlorn. "At least we found out all this before we sent our money in. We would have lost it."

I ended with, "So Dad says it's always wise to run stuff like this past grown-ups."

"I don't think they're that much smarter than kids," Bits grumped.

"No, but they've been around longer. They know more about life."

Bits made a messy noise. Then she said what I terribly, terribly hoped she would *not* say. "Oh, hey, guys. Mr. Smooth here"—she dipped her head toward me—"is a spearhead. Our youth director wants him to spearhead our youth group's fund-raising and help projects."

See? Didn't I tell you I should have kept my mouth shut last night? What happened was that the youth director collared me after the meeting and said he wanted me to help.

"That's great, Les!" Of course Lynn would think so. "Did you get any fund-raising ideas that the Sugar Creekers could use?"

"I don't know. They talked about an old-fashioned ice cream social and a bake sale and a car wash. The usual stuff."

"Hey, I know!" Bits waved her tofu sandwich. "A lemonade stand! The summer softball season's just starting. We set up out on the curb by Clothier Field and rake it in!"

Tiny frowned. "But they already sell lemonade inside. At the concession stand."

"So we knock some off the price they charge, and everybody will buy from us instead."

"I don't know." Lynn was the only one who seemed to eat tofu heartily. She probably grew up with it. "Do you think people comparison-shop at a ball game?"

"Lynn," Bits grumbled, "you're always the wet blanket, telling us why something won't work. You come up with something better."

"I'm trying."

"Well, until then, let's pool some funds and buy supplies. The opening games are tomorrow." Bits looked from face to face. "Everyone agreed?"

I shrugged. "Sure. I'll give it a shot."

Tiny didn't seem exactly thrilled. "We can try it."

And then Mike, looking like someone just stomped on his dog, said, "I can't help. I shoulda told you before, I guess. My dad got laid off, and Mom can't pick up many extra hours at her job. We're really short on money. There ain't no way I can save up for a new bike. Everything I make goes to help with the rent and groceries and stuff."

Bits muttered something about how much a kid can earn.

I didn't hear it exactly, but Mike must have. He said, "I earned fifty dollars just last week! Mom paid the light bill with it."

Bits's head snapped up. "How'd you make fifty bucks?"

"I worked for it. Hey, I want to help, really. I just can't. I'm sorry." And he sighed.

We were sorry, too. Here was the one who needed a bike the most, and he couldn't join in.

Talk about sorry. Let me summarize the next week of money-making efforts by the Sugar Creek Gang, because it's all too painful to describe in detail.

The lemonade stand was a zero hit with the public and lost us $2.84.

Tiny thought maybe a bake sale. When we burned the cookies, Mom chased us out of the kitchen. I admit the smell was pretty bad. But, hey, our smoke alarms work. Even the one in the basement.

We thought about writing a cookbook for kids and selling it door to door, but what if word got out about those cookies?

A week after we started, we had exactly

$6.00—15 percent of Lynn's allowance and 15 percent of that $20 I got for helping at the church. Tiny's contribution got eaten up in lemonade and cookie supplies.

And that's pretty sorry, if you ask me.

12

The next day, Lynn and I rode out to the animal shelter. It was a pleasant ride along mostly country roads, once you left the residential subdivisions.

I couldn't help but think about Mike—worry about him, in fact. He seemed to be separating himself from us. It was almost as if he felt guilty about something and didn't want to face us.

That silver bike seat worried me most of all.

Lynn cruised along right behind me. "The wildflowers are pretty now, aren't they?"

Well, frankly, I hadn't noticed them. But she was right. White daisy-like flowers and little yellow ones clustered in wide patches in the pastures.

Lynn quoted, "'See how the lilies of the field grow. They do not labor or spin. Yet I tell you that not even Solomon in all his splendor was dressed like one of these.'"

"Yeah. And I bet if rich old Solomon wanted a Gormann Super Roadmaster, he coulda bought one."

"Oh, honestly, Les!" But she was giggling.

We bounced and jostled back the rutted gravel lane to the shelter, and I thought how smooth the ride would be with the Roadmaster's front fork shocks and glide suspension seatpost. And comfort grips. Don't forget those.

We dumped our bikes by the door just as Tiny was pulling his empty coaster wagon back toward the reception room. He parked the wagon and led the way in.

I asked, "Mike isn't here today?"

"He's working for his brother. His big brother Joe has a lawn mowing service. When Mike helps, they get done faster and can take on special jobs."

"What kind of special jobs?" I was all ears. Here might be something the youth group could use.

Tiny recorded the feeding in the log book. "Oh, like this woman's holding her daughter's wedding in her backyard, and she wants the lawn trimmed the day before. She usually mows it herself, but she's too busy. And I guess some businesses don't use services regularly. They only call in somebody like Joe when the weeds out back are pretty high. That kind of thing, Mike says."

"Mm." I didn't see much potential there for either the youth group or the Creekers. "I wonder if that's how he made that fifty dollars last week that he talked about."

"I don't know."

Lynn was standing in the open door, idly looking out. "Here comes the garbage collector."

Tiny walked to the door frowning. "This isn't collection day."

I went over to watch the garbage truck, too, because there was not a solitary other thing to do around that place. It's pretty bad when a garbage truck is your big-ticket entertainment. I'd almost rather play computer games.

The truck brought in a shiny new Dumpster on its fork. It set the new bin down beside the old one. The two bins were quite a contrast —one brightly painted green, the other one faded, with scuffs and rust patches. The truck forked the old one up, lifted it high, and started to back up. Its backup beeper hooted.

Lynn bolted forward and ran toward the truck.

"Now what?" Tiny asked.

Lynn stood for a couple minutes at the driver side talking to the operator, her neck cricked way back because he was so high up. She waved good-bye and stepped back. The truck lumbered out the rutted gravel lane, the shabby old Dumpster bin clunking on its fork lift. Obviously deep in thought, Lynn came strolling back our way.

This wasn't a business meeting, since the only food was the birdseed and dog meal Tiny had just distributed on the wagon. But I reported anyway. "Lynn and I have been looking all over the neighborhood for work to do. You know—yard work, painting, stuff like that. *Nada.* Nobody wants to hire kids."

"Isn't Bits trying?"

"Nah. She stays home and fools around on her computer. Then she has the nerve to tell me, 'Why are you trying so hard? You're not making any more money than I am.'"

Tiny grinned—grimly. If you can grin that way. "Sounds like she's right. You know, we're going about this all wrong."

And I knew exactly what he was thinking, because I'd been thinking the same thing. "We're not getting anywhere because we haven't been praying about this."

"More than that. We're not seeking God's will."

Seeking God's will. You hear that all the time in Sunday school. Once in a while the pastor back in Seattle would preach about it. But it wasn't something you applied to little stuff (little from God's point of view, not mine) like buying a new bike. You "sought His will" for big things, like wars and what you do when you grow up.

I asked, "How do you find out what He wants?" though, of course, I already knew the answer.

"The Bible. And praying, but mostly the Bible. We haven't been doing that."

Lynn stepped in beside us and settled against a doorpost. "Haven't been doing what?"

"Seeking God's will about how to earn bike money."

"I have too. It's just that He hasn't suggested anything yet." The way she said it startled me. She was so matter-of-fact. She talked about God as if He lived in her upstairs bedroom. A regular person. A companion she'd chat with.

Tiny didn't give that impression exactly. But he was dead certain we were supposed to find out what God wanted in raising money as well as in wars and careers.

So that night at dinner, I asked Dad how to find things in the Bible. I mean, short of memorizing the whole thing.

He grinned. "I'll show you."

After supper we went to his den. "Have a seat, Les." He flopped into his big leather armchair on wheels, gave it a push backward, and raised his feet. The chair rolled across the room and drifted up against the bookcase on the far wall. He pulled a couple books off the shelf, turned half a turn, and rolled back to the desk.

He plopped one of his two books in my lap. "This is a concordance. It lists every word that's in the Bible and gives all the verses where the word occurs."

He handed me the second. "This is a topical Bible. It lists things by subjects—whether the subject is mentioned in the Bible by name or not. Then it gives all the verses that talk about that subject."

"What's the difference between subjects and words? Like, for instance, work is work."

"Well, let's see." He sat back. "Jesus, Paul, and others talk about Father, Son, and Holy Spirit. We call them the Trinity. The three in one. But the actual word 'Trinity' wasn't used until over a hundred years after the Bible was written. So the word 'Trinity' is not in the Bible, but the God we call the Trinity is."

"I see." I thumbed through them. In the

topical Bible, I opened by chance to the Fs. There was *fire*, with dozens of headings under it. *Elijah taken up in a chariot of* was one heading. Another entry stopped me cold. *an instrument of divine vengeance.* Surely God didn't take revenge on our church! Or did someone set fire to it, mistakenly thinking he was doing God a favor? People do some weird stuff like that, thinking they're doing what God wants, but they're not.

"Can I borrow these?" I asked, knowing the answer.

"Certainly."

I carried them off to my room and flopped on my bed. Tiny was right. We had to figure out God's will if we were going to get anywhere. Somehow, I would look up money-making methods that God would approve of.

I already knew the verse that says the love of money is the root of all kinds of evil. But I wasn't planning to fall in love with it. I just wanted to swap it for a Gormann Super Roadmaster.

13

A car wash is a big happy water fight without balloons. If you ever get a chance to help in one, do it. Just don't wear anything that can't get soaked, and that includes watches.

As the new spearhead at the youth group, I was supposed to hold a car wash as a money-maker. As I said, I had never been in a youth group before, let alone a car wash. But there was this kind of hoity-toity girl in the group who thought she was destined to be queen of the United States. She just might be, too. Her name was Diane Hargan. She was a year older than I was, and let's just say she didn't shop much in discount stores. She lived close to Sugar Creek Park in a ritzy part of town. Anyway, I asked her to run the wash because, I told her, she could do it better than anyone else.

Give the queen her due, she did a great job as chairman. Chairgirl. Chairperson. Chair. She arranged to hold it at a gas station on a busy corner. She planned every detail. Then she enlisted her mom to do the driving and buying things she'd forgotten, but she didn't forget many. We had signs, people in goofy costumes to dance around out by the street and yell, lots of soap, buckets, chamois, tar remover, bath towels, cleaner for the inside windows, and three of those little battery-driven vacuum things with rechargers. We plugged in the rechargers at the station.

When you got your car back, even the inside of the trunk was clean. I got a notion that maybe the queen was also nosy, because she insisted on vacuuming the trunks herself. It gave her a chance to look inside.

But I'm sure not criticizing. As we were winding down in late afternoon, she said, "We should give the gas station manager a thank-you present." She was right, so I said, "Go for it." At the grocery store nearby her mom bought a flower arrangement. I would never in a million years have thought of flowers, but the fellow seemed genuinely happy to get them. And he practically begged us to come back to his place and do it again.

We made a lot of money off that day of work, and almost all of it was pure profit. By the time we cleaned up and returned borrowed stuff, it was dark. Mom picked me up and took me home. I needed everything but a shower; I'd been sudsed and soaked all day.

She was feeding me my second helping of honey chicken and beans when Stan McCorkle, the youth pastor, stopped by. I heard Dad and him in the front room. Then here he came, swooping into the kitchen. He flopped into a chair across from me at the kitchen table before I had a chance to stand up. (Note: At our house, we kids have to rise when adults enter the room, or we get to eat our next supper standing up. Believe me, it's harder than it sounds.)

"Les, you were great! Do you know how much we made today?"

"Yes sir. Diane and I counted it."

He started telling Mom and Dad how this was the best fund-raiser they'd ever had, and on and on.

Another rule is, we're not supposed to interrupt adults. But finally, I did. "Sir? Sir! It wasn't me. Trust me. It was Diane. All of it was Diane. All I did was wash bugs off grilles. She planned the whole show and ran it, including the bouquet for the manager. She was brilliant at it."

"You're being way too modest."

"In fact, sir, she would be a much better spearheader. You ought to put her in charge instead of me."

You know, he didn't even hear that. He went on some more about how I delegated well and didn't let ego get in the way. When he stood up, I stood up. No fool, I. There was a good chance I could still eat supper tomorrow sitting down, and I wasn't going to spoil it.

He said good-bye to Mom and Dad, everyone shook hands, and I was asked to see him to the door.

Out on the front step, he turned to me and said, "Les, you're doing a great job! Keep up the good work."

"Thank you, sir."

"Not 'sir.' Call me Stan."

"Stan." So much for getting out of the spearheading. "Uh, Stan? One thing. How do you go about seeking God's will? Especially, seeking His will about making money."

He patted me on the shoulder. "Les, you don't have to worry the least little bit about that. You're doing fine!" And away he went.

It looked a lot like we Creekers were going to be on our own on this one. I wandered back to the kitchen and continued my appointment with the destiny of that honey chicken.

On her face, Mom had one of those *I'm proud of you, Son* smiles that she gets sometimes (well, actually, rarely). She popped me a soda to drink with dinner, and I didn't even ask for one. "Sounds like you're a real pro."

"Right. Professional fund-raiser."

She must have caught my tone of voice, because she said, "There are such people, you know."

"Aw, come on."

"Really. You'll find cheats and crooks in fund-raising, the same as in most other areas of life where money is involved. But there are also some very good ones, people who help organizations like our church raise thousands, even millions, of dollars. In fact, the church is considering hiring one."

"You pay a salary to a fund-raiser?"

"No. They charge either a fee or a percentage. Same as a stockbroker."

Professional fund-raiser. Whoever goes into high school saying, "I'm preparing to become a fund-raiser—it's my dream someday"? And yet, the need seemed to be there. Our church, for example. It might even be a great job, if you could somehow finance people's dreams.

Or, as in our church, repair damage. As the pastor at our old church in Seattle once said, "restore the years the locusts have eaten." That sort of thing. Not a bad career choice, when you think about it. Rewarding. Hard work, I bet. Maybe even fun.

Car washes are hard work and a lot of fun. But they sure aren't a career opportunity.

14

You know what I mean by buddy lists. Different carriers call it different things, but it's a computer program where you list the e-mail addresses of everyone you like to talk to. Then if one of those people logs on at the same time you're logged on, the screen tells you. The really great thing is that you can then switch over to a sort of private chat room of your own and type messages back and forth with this person that's on line with you. Some programs let you talk to each other live voice instead of typing to the screens, but not all of us had computers that could do that.

I figured maybe on the Web I'd find some answer to how to seek God's will without spending a whole lot of time trying. When I went on line to start a search, the buddy-list program flashed me the message that Bits, Lynn, and Tiny were all on. So this is how our typed-in conversation went (incidentally, who bothers with periods and stuff when you're talking? Capital letters do fine):

B [which is Bits]:   Hey Les you're on
M [that's me, Les]: Looks like all of us are
B: Tiny Is Mike with you
T: No Want me to get him

B: No I want to talk about him I heard daddy talking about church fire investig Suspicious origin Their looking for a Hispanic boy seen leaving the church and it sounds like Mike What do we do

L [Lynn]: They don't know it's arson

B: Yes they do Chem tests came back Oil where the fire started

M: You aren't supposed to talk about ongoing cases

B: But this is MIKE They even described his bike

T: Mike wouldn't do that

B: He might be in big trouble if they track him down What do we do

T: Meet at the creek now

L: Don't bring mike

T: I won't

Lynn, Bits and I rolled our bikes out onto the street at about the same moment—what Dad calls the immediacy of e-mail, I guess. When we got to the park's bike rack, Tiny's bike was already chained to it. I guess he lives closer than we do. We locked up and hurried down the trail and around the swamp loop.

Tiny stood on the creek bank with the water gurgling along inches from his shoes. Through his binoculars he was watching what looked to my unaided eye like a woodpecker up in the top of a tree on the other side of the creek. He turned when we arrived and slogged up the bank to settle with us at our favorite place. We call it the board room, that quiet, close little glade.

No food today. No intros or openers. But this was a business meeting, all the same—a serious one.

Bits began with, "This is what scares me. Daddy took a call in the kitchen this morning while we were eating breakfast. I think it was someone with the fire department. They talked awhile. I picked up the description when Daddy repeated it as he wrote it down. It sounds just like Mike. Even a green shirt like those shelter shirts you two wear."

"A million kids sound like Mike's description!" Tiny protested.

"A green T-shirt, Tiny! But that's not what scared me as much as this: At one point Daddy said, 'Oh, shoot, Harold, you can buy an arson for fifty bucks.'"

"So what?" Tiny looked just plain hostile.

"Don't you remember? Mike says he made exactly that much last week, but he wouldn't say how!"

We all just sat there silent awhile.

Then Lynn asked quietly, "And the bike sounded like his, too?"

"Yeah, with a silver seat. That could be his duct tape job."

Tiny glared at me. "What were you asking us a couple days ago about a metal seat?"

"I heard this description stuff then, but I'm not allowed to spill anything about a case in progress. Not a whisper. Bits, you blew it. You're not supposed to, either."

"Mind your own business." Bits doesn't take criticism well. But then I don't give it well.

More silence. We all just sat around staring at anything except each other, thinking, getting nowhere—at least, I was getting nowhere.

I thought about the horrible damage in the church, the dirt and smell and spoilage and all. An awful lot of money would go into fixing things, and the church needed that money so badly for other things. Not just the church suffered, but so did all the people the church had planned to help. If you fix up the church, you have to cut out a lot of other projects.

Even the youth group was affected. So were all the places the youth group would have paid money to on their outings. The YMCA swimming pool and skating rink we would have rented lost out. The people putting on the outdoor concert we would have gone to, and the book fair, and the zoo, and . . .

It was like tossing a stone into a fishpond. From where the stone hits the water, rings expand out, getting bigger and bigger, reaching farther, touching more and more things, and all from that one little *ploop* that started it all.

For fifty dollars.

Tiny looked right at Lynn. "What do we do?"

She licked her lips. "That's what I've been thinking about. We have a spectrum of choices."

Now that right there is why Tiny would ask

Lynn directly. Who else that you know can work the word *spectrum* into a conversation?

Lynn raised her right hand. "At one end, we simply turn him in. Tell the police what we know." She raised her left. "At the other end, we ignore it all and keep our noses out."

"That's my vote," Tiny interrupted.

"No!" Bits shook her head. "If you know about a crime and don't tell, it makes you an accessory. Accessories and felons get equal time. And arson is a felony. I say, get in his face and confront him."

I asked Lynn, "What's in the middle?"

"That's where I've been thinking. All we have is a suspicion. Like Tiny says, a lot of kids fit the description."

"Except for the bike with the metal seat," Bits said. "And the green shirt."

"Yes. Still, we don't really know anything. So I suggest we investigate some ourselves before we say anything outside the gang here. Then we'll know better whether Mike is involved. *Might* be involved, I mean."

And then, with heavy, heavy sadness in her voice, Lynn said to Tiny, "If he's guilty, Tiny, we can't protect him. That would only hurt him. If he sets fires—and some kids do—he needs help."

Tiny looked bleak, but then we all did. "Easy to say 'investigate,' but what do we do? What do we find out? What do we say?"

I, the long-time mystery reader, could answer that one. "We find out where he was that afternoon. You always place the suspect at the crime scene first. If he was somewhere else, that takes care of it right there."

Tiny stared a few moments at the dry leaves that were the carpet of our business office. He was closest to Mike. For years, he and Mike had shared the original Sugar Creek books because neither could afford them all. He had the most to lose.

Then he mumbled in that deep, dark voice, "We better start praying hard."

And nobody argued.

15

I got home from our business meeting at lunchtime. Mom had egg salad sandwiches waiting for me. She apparently had already eaten. I put extra mayo on mine—she tends to spread it a little thin—and added milk and an apple. I was just settling in when the doorbell rang.

I heard Mom's voice and the rumbling voice of a stranger. A moment later, Mom called me. I left behind sandwich and apple (reluctantly —I was hungry), chewing and swallowing and wiping my hands on my shirt on the way to the front room.

A very tall, very bulky, balding man in a suit and tie stood by the front door. Mom had obviously not invited him to sit.

She nodded toward me. "My son, Les. Les, this is Detective Joseph Chase with the police department."

"How do you do?" I reached for a handshake the way I'd been taught.

He was not into shaking hands with kids. He just stood there with his hands clasped in front of him. "Les, I understand you're friends with the boy who started that church fire."

Talk about a slam! He could've hit me with a brick and not stopped me so cold. What do you say?

Fortunately, I didn't have to say anything.

Mom dived right in. "Detective Chase, that was provocative at the very least. You are certainly welcome to sit down and talk to Les, but you will do it in the presence of his father." She walked over to the phone.

Detective Chase got testy right away. "Your son is not being accused, Mrs. Walker. He is not a suspect. He is—"

"He is eleven years old, Mr. Chase, and no match yet for an adult." Mom punched in Dad's cell phone number. "His father will be here in a matter of minutes, and you can proceed then. Les, go finish your lunch. Mr. Chase will wait."

The detective raised a ham-sized hand. "I prefer he not leave. Please. I don't want him calling up his little friends."

Mom looked uncertain about what to say and do, so I said, "It's OK. I'm not hungry anymore." I flopped into the Naugahyde recliner chair.

Mom nodded. She had Dad on the phone then, telling him to come home immediately. She hung up without giving him a reason. But I knew Dad wouldn't need a reason. If Mom said something like that, he'd be here instantly. Period.

The milk and egg salad I'd already eaten churned around down there, threatening to come back. I was scared like you wouldn't believe. When you read this kind of thing in a mystery story, it all just flows along. But in real life, it stops you cold, terrifying you.

He didn't say the boy we think might have started the church fire. He said the boy who did it. They must have gathered some kind of evidence pointing to Mike. We sat in silence as thick and heavy as wet cement.

I knew I was supposed to be praying like sixty right now, but I didn't know what to ask for or say. My mind was zip, like a car stuck in deep snow. The wheels would spin, the back end might wag a little from side to side, but it wasn't going anywhere.

What had poor old Mike got himself into?

I forgot to look at a clock to see when Mom called Dad, but it couldn't have been but a couple minutes and in the door he came. They introduced around, and Mom explained the situation to Dad in one short sentence: "He says Les knows the boy who set the church fire."

Dad's eyebrows rose. "Oh? They have a conviction already?"

Detective Chase rumbled, "Unless you're a lawyer, Mr. Walker . . ."

"As a matter of fact, I am." Dad handed the man his card.

And that right there changed the whole feeling in our living room. All of a sudden, Mr. Chase wasn't nearly as in-your-face as before. He still acted just as irritated as ever, but he seemed cautious now. The change was so sudden, it kind of took my mind off what was happening.

The whole session lasted an hour or so. Mr. Chase did not say again that my friend set the fire, so I figured maybe they didn't have evidence after all. And the reason he was here was that he was trying to find out Mike's full name and address.

Someone—who knows who—told the police that a kid of that description hung out with Bits and me sometimes. It had to be someone at our church who knew us but not Mike. They didn't know who Tiny was, either—at least, Mr. Chase didn't mention any tall, black kid, and you better believe I didn't either.

Mr. Chase kept asking me Mike's last name. And this is really crazy: I couldn't remember. Cross my heart I wasn't holding out. I would have told him if I could remember. But when I said my brain was a bogged-down car, I wasn't kidding. *Delgado* didn't sound right. *Alvarez* wasn't quite it. And I could not for the life of me dredge up what it was. Just so I didn't sound like a complete dummy, I explained that we didn't use last names much. Which was true.

He also asked me a dozen times where Mike lived. That one I could answer truthfully with "I don't know." I had never been to his house (or Tiny's either), and I had never heard the street address of either of them. With e-mail addresses, location has nothing to do with it. You can be talking to somebody next door or in Vermont or in South Africa. There's no way to tell.

And then Mr. Chase just sort of dismissed me from his life. He quit talking to me and talked to Mom and Dad instead, as if I weren't even there. "Your son is covering up," he said.

"I don't believe for a minute that he doesn't remember the boy's name. And his coverup suggests to me that he knows more about the boy's involvement than he's letting on."

Mom protested, and Mr. Chase cut her off with, "I know kids, Mrs. Walker. I'm an expert on children."

Well, now, you just don't say that to a schoolteacher, who really *is* an expert on children. Her voice turned to ice. "Is that so, Mr. Chase? I happen to be an expert on Les. He doesn't lie. If he says he doesn't remember, it is because he doesn't remember. Or never knew to start with. Before you weigh children against adult criteria, I strongly suggest you find out how children form relationships and what is important to them. And I assure you, last names and addresses are not important."

Mr. Chase's dark face told the world that he thought he was being flummoxed. *Flummox* was a word my grandmother used when she meant someone was pulling a fast one. He stood up suddenly and headed for the door. Mom and Dad followed him, said some kind of polite parting words, and closed the door behind him.

I flopped back in the chair and closed my eyes.

Dad stood by the chair arm. "Anything I should know here?"

I love the way Dad can accuse you without saying a solitary accusing word. I sat up again. "Mike has us worried. He's acting offish. Staying away from us. He says he has to help his brothers because his dad was laid off and they need money. And the description of the kid leaving the church fits him exactly. But he's a good kid, Dad."

Mom asked, "You really don't remember his name?"

"Mom, that Mr. Chase had me so confused I couldn't remember mine! And none of the Creekers except Tiny has ever been to his house. So we—"

Someone pounded on the front door. Dad raised an eyebrow. "Can't be Chase back."

It was Bits. When Dad opened the door, she roared in. "We just had a plainclothes at the house! And he was grilling *me!* He wanted to know Mike's name and address and how to get hold of him and everything."

I sighed. "Welcome to the club."

16

Dad sat at the kitchen table with his coat off and his tie loose, munching cookies. Mom sat at the table just as relaxed, sipping tea. Bits and I were chowing down cookies and milk. My stomach might have been doing flips fifteen minutes ago, but now that Mr. Chase was gone, it was ready to take on more grub.

"So I played dumb." Bits continued her story. "I said I didn't remember Mike's last name, and it's true that I don't know where he lives."

Dad had a half smile. "Why didn't you want to cooperate, Bits?"

"'Cause Daddy says don't ever do anything like that unless he's there. He was at work, and I couldn't reach him. And Mrs. Grimes, who baby-sits me and cleans the house, is clueless. Zippo. So I told the detective, 'I don't say anything without my dad, so see him. Maybe he can help you.' And he left. He left mad, but he left."

So Detective Chase tried to talk to both of us and didn't get anywhere. If I ever became a police officer when I grew up, I would sure go about interrogations differently. Bet I'd have more success, too.

Mom made a face. "'I know kids. I'm an

expert.' In a pig's eye he is." Obviously, that still really irritated her.

I sighed. "I'm ashamed of this, Dad, but I can remember his name now. Alvarado. I really couldn't remember then. Really!"

Mom smiled. "Not something to be ashamed of, Les. When you're flustered, that kind of thing often happens. If Mr. Chase really were an expert, he'd know that and expect it to happen and do his best to relax you. Instead, he seemed to be doing his best to fluster you."

Bits's mouth had crumbs around the edges. "But I still don't know where Mike lives. Do you?"

I shook my head. "Bet we could find out, though." I hopped up and fetched the phone book. There had to be a dozen Alvarados. More.

Bits said, "Keep your finger in that spot and look up Wilson. Then we match addresses, Alvarados and Wilsons, until two are close. That'll be Mike and Tiny."

Brilliant!

We had his address in less than three minutes.

"Now what are we going to do with it?" I asked. "Give it to the police?"

Dad stared off into space for a while. "Bits, we'll give it to your father when he gets home. I suggest not dealing with Detective Chase unless we must. I got the strong impression that he assumes Mike is guilty. In fact, as I listened to our Mr. Chase, I think you two are under suspicion, also. As accomplices if not more."

"But we found the fire!" Bits exclaimed.

"Arsonists frequently turn the alarm in. Professional firebugs don't, but amateurs do. They often hang around to watch too."

Bits stuck her wrists out. "Well, you might as well just snap the cuffs on. Try to do a good deed! Honestly."

Dad went back to work then, after warning both of us not to talk to police or anybody else without either Sergeant Ware or him sitting in. Mom went back to what she'd been doing.

Bits was going to go back to her computer games, but I threatened to throw the main junction box switch and cut off all the power to her house. We called Lynn and invited her along. Then, armed with an address now, we three went out to find Mike Alvarado.

The Alvarado house was a really nice place. A great place, even. It had a second story (I love houses with stairs) and a lot of shady trees in the yard, including an apple tree that looked perfect to climb.

We knocked at the door, and a sturdy woman answered. She wasn't fat. She was sturdy—square and strong-looking, with long hair pulled back into a bun.

"We're friends of Mike's, ma'am. Can he come out?"

She smiled, warm and cheery. "You look like his Sugar Creek Gang. Are you?" Her accent was so thick it was hard to understand.

She nodded when we did. "Mike, he is with

his brothers, but they will be back soon. They get a bite and then go out again."

So we sat on the porch and listened to the robins complain about the poor quality of worms —or whatever it is that robins chirp about.

Mike and his brothers arrived in a battered pickup about half an hour later. Mike, a brother about twelve, and a brother old enough to drive all got out.

Mike's grin would have covered a king-size bedspread. "What you guys doing here? Mama give you ice tea, yet?"

Lynn nodded. "She offered."

I said, "You look pooped, man." And he sure did, too. Sweaty, dirty, and droopy.

"Day ain't over." Mike flopped down on the porch step beside us. "We got our lawns done, but Joe has two other jobs lined up yet."

Bits pointed. "That Joe's truck?"

"Yeah. Dad is out in his own truck. Since he ain't working, he been helping Joe do lawns and stuff, too. He should be in soon."

I was trying to figure out how to sneak up on the subject we really wanted to talk about: where Mike was when the church caught fire.

Good old Bits didn't sneak. She just jumped right into the middle. "You remember when our church burned?"

"Yeah." Mike paused. His mom appeared in the doorway, handed him a tall glass of iced tea with no ice in it, and went back inside. He sipped. "I saw it on TV that night—the ten o'clock news—and I remember thinking, 'Hey, that's Bits and Les's church!'" He leaned back against the porch post.

"So where were you that afternoon?"

Lynn closed her eyes and kind of wagged her head.

Mike didn't seem nervous about the question. "Hadda go to the library. I had an over-due book. I wanted to pay it before the fine got any bigger, y'know?" His eyes got wide. "Hey! You know what? I went right by that church almost 'zactly the time it caught fire!"

17

So there we had it. Now we knew. Mike was in the right place at the right time. Or wrong time, if you prefer. The witnesses who saw the kid at the church were seeing Mike. I didn't know about Lynn and Bits, but my brain was a muddle. Now what?

Tiny came rolling down the sidewalk on his bike. When he reached us, he dragged both feet. That was how he always slowed down or stopped when he wasn't going very fast. His brakes weren't real good.

He was wearing the green shelter T-shirt, so he must have just come off work. He pulled into the yard, spilled his bike, and flopped down on the porch with us. "Hey! What's happening?"

Bits waved a hand. "You see it all right here."

Mike's brother walked by, toting two big gas cans—ten gallons or bigger. I mean *big*. They seemed lightweight, probably empties. He was taking them back to a shed. A few moments later, here he came back again with two very heavy cans. He humped them up into the bed of the pickup and went into the house. If they burned that much gasoline mowing lawns, they had mowed a whole lot of lawns that day.

Then Joe slammed the screen door open

and stood in the doorway with his hand over the receiver of a phone on a long cord. "You guys wanna have some fun and make a little money?"

Bits sat up straighter. "Doing what?"

"Lots of fun. I got this fellow needs a big job done in two hours. I don't wanna turn him down—the money's real good—but we got two other jobs going already. I don't have the warm bodies, unless you help."

I shrugged. "Sure. I'll go."

Lynn, Tiny, and Bits nodded.

Joe's grin spread reassuringly wide. He said to the phone, "Yessir, Mr. Becker, we can do it. At that price." After a pause, "Thank *you*, sir!" He hung up and called back into the house, *"See, Mama! Poe-day-muss ah ah-sare-lo! Odd yose."* Or whatever that is in Spanish. I really ought to learn Spanish sometime.

So we all piled into the back of the pickup truck, and Joe took us out to a lumber mill on the east side of town. I'd never ridden like that before—you know, clear out in the open. Believe me, it's a lot more fun to ride in the rear of a pickup than in the backseat of an air-conditioned sedan.

We laughed and talked and tried to keep the swirling wind from kicking dust into our eyes. When we got there, Bits's ponytail looked as if it had been through a wind tunnel backwards.

The mill operator didn't say it in so many words, but I gathered that he was going to get a "surprise" visit early in the morning from a safety inspector of some kind. And his place was a mess. He looked disappointed—even angry—when a bunch of kids jumped down from the back of Joe's pickup.

But Joe raised a hand. "Wait'll you see, Mr. Becker. We do good work!"

"Hmph. It better be worth the price I'm paying."

And it was! Joe and Mike and their brother, with scoop shovels and wheelbarrows, moved huge piles of sawdust and shavings and shredded bark from the yard to the incinerator. With big paint brushes, Bits and I dusted off the giant saws and other power tools. We'd start at the top and just brush to the bottom, reaching in small places as best we could. Next we wiped them down with an oily rag. Then Lynn came along and cleaned up the piles of gunk we'd made. Lynn and Tiny cleared the big spaces between tools with push brooms.

The regular mill crew worked, too, but mostly they stacked and sorted lumber that was lying all over. They put away the hand tools lying here and there.

We finished in an hour and a half. Mr. Becker seemed satisfied, because he paid the full amount to Joe instantly. But even more, he seemed surprised. I bet he didn't think a bunch of kids could do all that so well so fast. And that, let me tell you, really pleased us. All of us. I know I felt smug. No, not smug. Proud.

Did Mike and his brothers feel that same

pride when they finished a job well? I hope they did.

I found out almost by accident that Tiny helped them like that every once in a while and wouldn't take any money for it. We rode back to their house, and Joe handed the money to his mom. When she started to pay us, we refused to accept anything. I was going to do that anyway, and I'm happy that Bits and Lynn had the same idea. We hadn't talked it over or anything. The mother insisted. We insisted. She let us win.

She didn't lose her cheeriness, but her eyes seemed wet. "This makes the rent payment. I don't know how to tell you how grateful we are. We didn't have enough until this job."

"But we just did a little bit," Lynn protested. "A couple hours' work. Not even that."

Joe shrugged. "Maybe. But it made all the difference. I'm grateful, too. It's pretty hard for us right now. You guys are great."

Biking home that evening, I thought a lot. I'd learned a couple of things that afternoon.

One, when stuff is dirty enough that you can see a big difference when you clean it, it makes you feel happy. I guess what I'm saying is it's very satisfying. Hey, those saws and things looked *good*. You could even tell what color they were. You couldn't before.

But the big thing I learned was how hard some work is. Sure, I did chores around the house and mowed the lawn and stuff like that. Compared to this, that wasn't much work. And then I thought about Mike, who had been doing this heavy stuff all day. He was tired when we started. I was tired in less than two hours, and he was younger than I. He must have been totally wiped.

I also thought how big fifty dollars must look to a kid who had to work that hard every day. Could Mike have hired himself out as an arsonist? I'm sure not saying maybe it was OK. Doing wrong never is. But I was beginning to see what a temptation something like that could be.

And doing wrong to get food and rent money is a whole lot more of a temptation than doing wrong to buy any Gormann Super Roadmaster.

18

How many times has Mom said to me, "It's not polite to eavesdrop!"?

Many, because . . . well, think about it. Here I have two sisters, both older, both very nosy about other people's business. They would surely eavesdrop on *me* if they thought I ever did anything worth knowing about. So I consider it an act of self-defense when I eavesdrop on them. Besides, it's fun to tease them about what I just happen to accidentally overhear from time to time.

It had never occurred to me that maybe, if you eavesdrop, you'll hear something you don't want to hear. But that's what happened to me the next day.

I told Mom where I was going and went over to visit Bits. But she was all wrapped up in one of her games, and I got bored, so I came back home and holed up in my room to work on an airplane model. I thought once about becoming a pilot.

When the doorbell rang, I didn't think much about it. I heard Mom answer the door. And then I thought I heard that Detective Chase. I was all ears instantly.

I left my room and tiptoed silently down the hall. I stepped into the open door of the guest bedroom, which is near the living room. From there you can hear almost anything going on in the front of the house.

I'm guessing that he asked if I was there, and Mom said no, because she didn't know I had returned. Then Mr. Chase said, "We'd like to look around in his room, in your shed out back, in the basement, and in the garage. You do have a basement, is that correct?"

"For that, Mr. Chase, you need a search warrant."

"Right here."

Mom: "Please be seated, both of you, while I read this."

So there were two of them. Why in the world would they want to look in my room? I got an icy scare-chill in my chest.

Finally, Mom said, "This clearly specifies where you may look and what you are seeking. I trust I won't have to remind you about straying from the guidelines here."

And Mr. Chase replied, very sarcastically, "We'll be good, ma'am." I'm betting he didn't like her any more than she liked him.

I stayed stone still as they came down the hall past the guest room. They went into my room in back with Mom right on their heels. I finally got the nerve to peek out. She was standing in my doorway. I couldn't see what they were doing.

I went back into hiding, tucking myself behind the chest of drawers in the guest room. When they came out, one went to the basement and the other into the garage. Then they trooped outside with Mom right behind them. Pretty soon they came back in.

Mom said, "What I want to know is why you consider my son an arsonist."

"Ma'am, he is a person of interest, but then so is—"

"No. He's a suspect. I can tell from what the warrant says and does not say. Now, please answer my question."

I was proud of Mom! Incredibly proud. She didn't let them scare her or back her down for a moment.

"Mrs. Walker, do you really believe that an eleven-year-old boy just happens to recognize wood smoke as he's riding down the street, and then follows his nose to a structure fire? Children are not that alert to their surroundings."

Mom started to say something.

He cut her off. "At one point in my prior interview, your husband said he did not coach the two children at the fire scene. And yet they knew exactly what to do. Kids don't think about hosing down a maintenance shed, Mrs. Walker. They just don't. And especially not on the spur of the moment like that."

"And as you've said, you know kids. You're an expert." I could tell from her tone of voice that Mom was mad.

"Besides, kids are selfish, thoughtless little monsters. They don't care about others. Your son was covering up for his playmate, and he wouldn't think to do that unless his playmate could somehow incriminate *him*."

And, boy, did Mom let fly. "Of all the nonsense! Mr. Chase, become a teacher. Perhaps twelve years' experience in the classroom will teach you, as it taught me, how sharp and how caring children can be. And how loyal. Your 'expertise' is woefully inadequate for truly understanding children. I'll let my husband know you were here. And of course, I'll tell my little monster, the arson suspect, that you're thinking of him. You may leave now."

You may leave now. If the queen of England heard that, and heard the way Mom said it, she would have left immediately. Mr. Chase and that other man sure did. I heard the door close. I moved over to the guest room window and watched through the filmy curtains as the police car pulled away from the curb.

And across the street at Bits's house, a car just like it waited at her curb. The front door of Bits's house opened. Mrs. Grimes appeared, looking really flustered, her hands dancing nervously. A woman and man came out the door. On the porch, they turned to talk to her a few moments. Then they got in their car and left.

I didn't see Bits. And I wondered, *Is she hiding, too?* Or was she so involved in her stupid game that she didn't care if they searched her house?

19

It had been six hours since Mr. Chase left our house, and Mom was still furious. She got mad at me once in a while but nothing like this. She sat at the kitchen table with a glass of iced tea in front of her, but she wasn't drinking it.

Dad was just as angry. He sat across from her, stewing.

Bits's father, Sergeant Ware, sat at one end, and Bits and I were there, too. It was not a happy group.

Dad looked at Bits and me. "Under no circumstances do you answer any question whatever from a police officer. Understood? You refer them to one of us." Him or Sergeant Ware.

"Yes sir." I felt like a rooster in a chicken factory, waiting and wondering when the ax would fall. "Do they really think Bits and I are suspects?"

Sergeant Ware nodded. "They don't go to the trouble of getting a warrant and tossing a place for the fun of it. They were fully expecting to find the kind of burglary tools and firebomb materials an arsonist would hide."

I sighed. "You realize, Dad, this sure blows what you've always said."

"Which is . . ."

"'Go to the cops first if you have a problem. They're your friends. They'll help.'"

Sergeant Ware smiled. "So your Dad told you that, did he? Well, it's true. You *can* still trust them. Especially if you're in trouble or danger. That hasn't changed."

"Oh, yeah?" Bits shot back. "Then why are they trying to put us in jail?"

Her dad leaned forward, both elbows on the table. "I did a little snooping. That is, I checked up on Detective Joseph Chase. As you know, officers take classes now and then to learn new skills—or refresher courses to sharpen skills. I do. Everyone does.

"Detective Chase attended a weekend workshop on juvenile criminals last year. Murderers, burglars, arsonists fifteen years old and younger."

Mom snorted. "And that makes him an expert?"

"Probably he thinks so. I know that workshop. The guy who teaches it is a juvenile officer who rarely sees a normal kid—a kid who doesn't get into trouble. All he sees are troubled kids. So he has a kind of prejudiced outlook. Doesn't see much good in kids because he doesn't see any good kids."

Mom nodded. "I can understand that. Now that you explain it, that's the way Detective Chase sounds. 'All children are monsters.'"

I'd read a lot of mysteries but never about arson before. "So what were they looking for exactly, besides burglar tools to break in some-where with?"

"Things to make fires burn fast and quick. For instance, if you have a gas-engine lawn mower, it's expected that you have a couple gal-lons of gasoline stored somewhere. But when you've got twenty gallons of gas out in the shed, it raises eyebrows."

I know my eyebrows sure went up. I looked at Bits. She shook her head, just plain grim.

Dad asked, "What?" and Sergeant Ware was looking at us.

Mom said, "Spill it. This is no time to hold back."

"Mike Alvarado went right by the church at about the time of the fire. We know because we asked him. And they have all these full gas cans in their shed. Big cans."

Bits told them then how we went out there and helped the Alvarados finish that special job. I could hear in her the same pride I had felt that we'd done something worthwhile and we'd done it well. And she told what we saw and how the Alvarado family needed money.

I finished it with, "But you know Mike. He isn't like that. He even wants to be a cop when he grows up. And it's sort of normal for them to have that much gas around, with all the power tools they use. They have gas trimmers too. And garden tillers. It doesn't mean any-thing." And then I remembered the correct word. "It's all circumstantial, right?"

"Right," Bits's dad agreed. "But if you're

looking for reasons to suspect someone, Mike would provide a lot of them." Then he just sat there, chewing on his lip. Bits said he was thinking when he did that.

Just then Catherine and Hannah came through the front door in a cloud of noise. Chattering like jackhammers, they showed Mom and Dad the twenty-dollar bill they'd earned baby-sitting, and I thought about the Gormann Super Roadmaster. Somehow, with all this arson business, the bike didn't seem so important.

And yet, it did. I still wanted one just as much as ever, but it was looking less and less like I'd ever get it.

The girls went back to their rooms, still jabbering.

Then Sergeant Ware said, "Let's go talk to Mike, Bill. Nothing official. Want to?"

Dad nodded. "Sure."

Sergeant Ware stood up. "You kids can come along."

So Bits and I went with them. We took Dad's car. I tried to think why they'd let us come, and then I remembered what Mom had said about helping kids feel relaxed.

Mrs. Alvarado was home, although the father hadn't gotten back yet. Bits and I introduced everyone, and she invited us to the kitchen. Mike and Joe sat at the kitchen table eating bacon and scrambled eggs.

Mrs. Alvarado said, "They get a little bite in the afternoon, and then they can work till dark. We're so lucky school is out, so that the boys can all help. Sit. Please sit. May I get you some cold tea?" I'm glad she didn't say *iced* tea, because she didn't put ice in it.

She didn't wait for a yes. She just poured. She even gave Bits and me tea. Apparently everyone who stepped in under that roof got tea.

Joe finished off the last of his snack and stood up. "I'll go load up the truck," and he left through the back door.

Sergeant Ware said, *"See enta say Tom byen, sen yora, por fuh vor,"* and Mrs. Alvarado sat down at the table. So he spoke Spanish. I really have to learn that language.

The sergeant smiled at Mike. "We're looking for people who saw something the evening of that church fire. Anything. Now, very often people don't realize that they've seen something that might be helpful. They don't know they have important information, in other words. And Bits mentioned that you went by there. So I'd like to ask you some questions."

"Sure." Mike seemed just plain eager. As I said before, he wanted to be a police officer, and here was a real police officer asking him real, official questions. He was glowing.

"Did you just go by, or did you stop anywhere around there?"

"I stopped. They have this bench out front, you remember? Sort of like a park bench, by some bushes. My bike chain jumped the sprocket again. It does that a lot. And there was this big slab of concrete in front of the bench, you know?"

Jim nodded. "So you had someplace to put the chain back on without turning your bike upside down on the sidewalk."

"'Zackly. I know how to do it now, so it only took a couple minutes, you know. Then I had to really hurry, because I ain't allowed out after dark and it was almost dark."

"Your chain work OK when you left?"

"Fine."

"Did you go around back at all?"

"No. Just the bench there."

"Hey, I hear your bike broke. Can I see it?"

"Sure." Mike led the way out to the shed. I knew when I saw Sergeant Ware looking all around that he was searching with his eyes for suspicious stuff. Six big gas cans lined the wall.

Dad and Jim Ware wagged their heads over the bike-in-two-pieces and agreed it would be hard to fix, if at all. The sergeant spent maybe ten or fifteen minutes more asking questions— did anyone else come by, did Mike see any cars stop, that kind of stuff.

I compared him to Mr. Chase, and there wasn't any comparison. The officer crooned along so smooth and casual, asking things that didn't matter and them slipping in something that did. Mike never seemed to be on his guard, the way I felt the whole time Mr. Chase was peppering me. If Detective Chase had been this good, I might even have remembered Mike's last name.

Then Dad and Sergeant Ware stopped by the kitchen to thank Mrs. Alvarado for her hospitality, and we headed out. So did Mike. He ran over and hopped into the back of Joe's pickup. They took off, no doubt headed for more hard work.

As soon as we were in the car and out on the street, Dad asked the sergeant, "How did he look to you?"

"Clean. Body language, responses, all look good. His story meshes exactly with the two witnesses who saw the child ride away. And his chain and sprocket are badly worn. Did you notice?"

"The whole bike is worn."

"Dad?" I asked from the backseat. "Would you represent him if he needed a lawyer?"

Dad nodded. "I'm satisfied he's innocent and telling the truth. But like you said, circumstantial evidence. To a very suspicious person like Detective Chase, the Sugar Creek Gang could be in the arson business."

20

I was broke. If you like British slang, I was flat. If you prefer French, *sans lucre*. Latin? Impecunious. In any language, I didn't have any money.

The youth of our church had unanimously pledged a tenth of all they made. Of course I, the spearhead, had to tithe and then some to set the example. That Sunday at church I put my pledge (I admit, reluctantly) in the special plate they passed for fire-rebuilding donations. So did all the other kids and many of the adults. Between promising part of my allowance to the church as a regular tithe and another part for the rebuilding fund, and the chunk I set aside for the bike, it was a waste of time to mend holes in my pockets. I had nothing to put in them anyway.

Caught up in the thrill of victory, Diane Hargan stood up and announced more fundraisers. Because the car wash was such a success, I had turned it all over to her. It was one of the smartest moves I ever made. She was really in her element, handling big ideas and big money. And she was doing a lot better than I ever could have. Besides, who wants to do that stuff? Not I.

The carpets were clean (and not moldy,

either!), but the church still smelled like burned wood. In short, it seemed almost normal, but not normal. Know what I mean? And I wondered if it would ever be normal again.

I was still thinking about that when pastor Earnhart's announcement snapped me to attention: "Several weeks ago, a car ran a stop sign near here and crashed into a pickup truck. Three children on bikes witnessed the accident and helped at the scene. The driver of the car is trying to find those children. If any of you know anything about it, see me afterwards for a number to call."

I looked up at Dad and whispered, "You do it, huh?"

He nodded.

And the service continued.

Later that afternoon, the Sugar Creek Gang met at the park. We couldn't make it a lunch meeting, because Tiny and Mike both had to go with their families to a Sunday-after-church lunch. So we made it an afternoon-snack meeting instead.

The creek bank at our favorite place seemed nicer than ever, I guess because I hadn't been there for a while. The shade felt cooler, the leaves greener and rustlier, the water burblier —you see what I mean. Some white puffy clouds were starting to get dirty bottoms, so it would probably rain soon, but for now the world looked bright.

Even though it was supposed to be only a snack, Tiny's mom had sent some sandwiches

—tuna salad, really good, with lots of mustard. Lynn brought apples and Bits oranges, Mike brought chips, and I poured lemonade all around.

I didn't even have my sandwich unwrapped yet when I spilled the news. "Lynn? Tiny? Remember when that car plowed into a pickup right in front of us?" I had their attention. "Well, the lady who ran the stop sign doesn't know who we are, and she's trying to find us. Dad's checking into it."

"Cool." Tiny lifted the bread to examine the interior of his sandwich. "How'd you find out?"

"The pastor read an announcement in church."

"They had an article about the accident in the paper the next day, but it didn't mention us." Lynn paused from devouring an apple. "I don't get it. Why not just call her up?"

"Because it could be a scam," Bits explained. "What if she wants to sue you for hurting her baby?"

"But I didn't!"

"That doesn't make any difference. I said 'scam.'"

A titmouse perched on a branch out over the water and made its funny chirping sound. We all knew what it was, thanks to Tiny.

Next I reported, "I've been thumbing through the Bible with a couple reference books, trying to find God's will about earning money. I can't find anything. I get a lot of stuff, but I can't find anything that fits except 'The workman is worthy of his hire.' Doesn't say what the workman should and shouldn't be doing, though."

"Well, don't worry about it," Bits said. "That car wash pulled in some big bucks. And, I mean, it's the church group. The pastor approved and everything. The car wash must have been God's will, right? So I think we Creekers ought to have a car wash, too. We'd make our bike money in no time."

Tiny frowned. "Our softball team held a car wash this spring. We made a little, but it was sure nothing to write songs about. How come you did so well?"

"Because people like their cars clean. Why else?" Bits stuffed her orange peels in the trash bag.

"Let's think about this," said Lynn. "Everybody in town knows about the church fire. So lots of your customers may have come to your car wash just to help the church. I mean, you may have had a big sympathy factor working in your favor."

"And you're saying," I translated, "that the Sugar Creek Gang doesn't get any sympathy."

She smiled. "Something like that. We certainly wouldn't have the kind of draw that a fire-damaged church does."

"Lynn," Bits grumped, "every time someone has an idea, you tell us why it won't work. Let's hear *your* brilliant plan."

"Problem is," said Tiny, "she always turns out to be right."

"Actually, I think I do have a good plan," Lynn said. "Tiny, remember when the garbage collectors brought that new Dumpster to the shelter?"

"Yeah. But it wasn't new, after all. It was just an old one with the outside cleaned and painted. The inside wasn't touched. Same old rust and gunk in there."

"I talked to the driver, remember, and he gave me a lot of useful information. The manager at that sawmill we helped clean up said we work better than some grown-ups. Remember? So the next day, I asked him to give us a letter of recommendation, and he did. Then my father and I called up the sanitation department."

I frowned. "You called up the *garbage collectors?*"

Bits shook her head. "I can't keep track of what you're talking about."

That didn't slow Lynn down a bit. "Then I made some calculations. My father thinks it should work very well. If each of us puts seven dollars into a fund for paint and supplies—I wasn't including you in this, Mike—we can make ourselves enough money to buy the bikes."

21

Sometimes I think Bits tries extra hard to be grumpy. You can't be that good at it unless you practice. As our business meeting in the park rolled along, she started yammering at Lynn. "Why should we sink a lot of money into paint? We won't make any money painting house numbers on curbs. Believe me. The Girl Scouts went through town putting house numbers on curbs a year ago, and the cheerleading squad tried the same thing this spring and didn't get any business. All the curbs are painted already. We have to think of something that hasn't been done a million times, and I'm telling you, that isn't it."

"Not house numbers." Lynn stashed her apple core in her daypack. "Dumpster bins."

Bits made a noise through her nose. "Somebody already paints them!"

"Right. That's what I talked to the driver about. Look. Right now, they have to haul a rusty bin back to their shop, wire brush it, paint it, put the sanitation department's number back on it, and haul it out onto a site again. Every single Dumpster. By the time they get done with the hundreds of Dumpster bins they own, the city has to start over because the first ones are scuffed."

"I see!" I just about cheered. "All that moving bins and hauling them around costs the city a body part. So along comes the Sugar Creek Gang to repaint the Dumpster right where it's sitting!"

"For half the money it would cost them to do it themselves." Lynn grinned. "Exactly!" She yanked a notebook out of her pack. "My father and I factored in the cost of paint, tools like wire brushes and paint sprayer and . . ."

Tiny's eyes got wide. "We'd have to buy a compressor and everything?"

"My father wants a compressor, anyway. He says he'll go buy it and let us use it, but it will be his. You just about need it to do a lot of Dumpsters in a short time—"

"Without brush marks. And we'd spray-paint the numbers with a stencil." I was really getting into this idea. Then I happened to glance at Mike.

He looked totally, droopy sad. It wasn't but a couple more minutes before he said, "Well, gotta get back. Joe wants to haul some construction trash yet this afternoon. See ya."

When he'd gone, Lynn made a face. "I don't want to leave him out, but it wouldn't be right to ask him to help us."

"I agree," I said. "Not when he works so hard already, and he wouldn't be able to save up for a bike anyway."

Then we broke up to go home. I pedaled back to my house, thinking how hard I didn't have to work. When I passed our church, that vague fire smell still lingered.

Lynn and her dad and my dad went over the plan she'd drawn up. And they helped us out a lot by going along with us when we went to talk to the sanitation department people about the Dumpsters.

The city manager was going to just shoo us out. I know he was. So was the maintenance supervisor.

You know how you can tell when a grown-up dismisses you as nothing? Well, the city manager said he had to let out that kind of maintenance thing on bids and contracts, and he even stood up to show us out the door. But Dad knows all about that, and he whipped out exactly the right kind of contract—I forget the name of it. Anyway, you sign this agreement to see if a new idea is going to work out, and then if the idea does work, you put it out on competitive bid and blah, blah, blah . . . I'm sure glad he was along, because I didn't understand a thing.

The supervisor insisted on ten Dumpsters as an experiment. Dad said twenty-five would be a better trial. Ten. Period. So ten it was. Dad and Mr. Wing reluctantly agreed, since that was the best they could get.

Mr. Wing bought himself an air compressor and showed us how to use it. We bought all the supplies, even the face masks so you don't breathe paint droplets. We dug out the oldest, rattiest clothes we owned, because in another day or two they were going to be green.

Mr. Wing, incidentally, is the nicest man. He's short and stocky and very, very quiet. Even when he's talking, his voice doesn't make much noise. And he doesn't talk much. But when he does say something, you'd better be listening, because it's something you ought to know. Come to think about it, that was exactly how Lynn is, too.

Know where the first trial Dumpster was? Sugar Creek Park! It's a county park, but since it's in town, the city handles the trash and maintenance. This, Dad said, was more "interagency contract stuff." And he explained a lot more than I was interested in knowing. All I wanted to know was which Dumpster to paint first.

We wire brushed every inch of rust on that sucker, and there were a lot of rusty inches. We took tar off with tar remover and washed it with soap and water. This was sure a lot more fun than a car wash!

Then came the exciting part—spray-painting it. We took turns. After a lot of fumbling around and time-wasting to make it work, we got the air compressor running. We hooked up the paint sprayer. Tiny went first and painted around the top. Next I tried it, and Bits yelled at me to quit making dribbles. Then she came along and made a couple of dribbles. Lynn quietly wiped all our drips off with a paper towel and took her turn with the sprayer. The paint dried in twenty minutes.

The maintenance supervisor had loaned us

a set of the stencils they wanted us to use. Bits held the stencil in exactly the spot they wanted, and Lynn sprayed on the white paint. That put the sanitation department logo and number on. With black paint we stenciled on the *DO NOT PLAY ON OR NEAR* warnings.

And it was done! Bright green, like new on the outside, and it hadn't moved an inch. I don't mind saying it looked good!

It had taken us almost four hours, but Lynn thought that as we did more of them and got better at it, it would go faster. I mentioned too that if we ever figured out how the sprayer worked, it would save time.

The maintenance supervisor himself came out to check the results. He pointed out things we should do differently, but he seemed more pleased than I thought he would be.

One down, nine to go! We were on our way to fame and fortune. And new bikes.

22

I am not usually one who notices that it's a beautiful day, or that the lilacs are coming into bloom, or that Mom just washed the kitchen floor, any of that kind of stuff. But this morning really *splacked* you right in the face with how perfect it was. Blue sky, warm breeze but not hot. Lynn and I decided to go bicycling down to the rescue shelter. We knocked on Bits's door and invited her, but she was wrapped up in something on her computer.

We were just getting back on our bikes when she stuck her head out her front door. "Wait up!" I thought she'd changed her mind, but apparently Mrs. Grimes had changed it for her and kicked her out of the house.

I know that's what happened, because, as Bits came out onto the porch with a pout on her face, the baby-sitter/housekeeper was saying ". . . too nice to be inside."

Bits hauled her bike out of their garage. "Got an e-mail just as I was leaving. Mike's going to help at the shelter this morning, so he rode out there with Tiny. Tiny said that detective was talking to Mike and his parents again, and Mike's pretty upset."

I'd be upset, too, if the detective was Mr. Chase or anyone like him. I thought about how much Mike wanted to become a police officer. If arson showed up on his record—or even worse, if he was actually guilty—that might destroy his career chances. One little thing could wreck his plans for his life.

Away we went. We probably looked more like a herd than a gang as we rode single file down the back streets and out into the country. Tiny had said yesterday that hikers found a badly mauled squirrel in Sugar Creek Park. Probably, dogs did it. So we were going out to visit the squirrel.

Besides, we had just finished up Dumpster number ten to complete our special contract with the city. Dad and Mr. Wing agreed that the city was never in a rush to pay its bills. So if the check didn't come when we needed it, they would advance us the money. We'd pay them back when the check arrived.

But we hadn't earned nearly enough from that job to buy anything just yet.

As soon as we got to the shelter, I began scooping feed for the rabbits and squirrels, while I explained, "My dad and Bits's dad found out about that woman who was in the accident. They both think everything's all right with her. She just wants us to get together for lunch sometime. Don't know when."

"Did she seem sorry that she caused the accident?" Bits asked.

"I don't know. But she told how it happened. She flat out didn't see the stop sign. Blew right through it, forgetting it was there.

She was looking down at her radio for just a second to change stations. And *bam!* That fast!"

Lynn wagged her head sadly. "Such a little thing, so much damage."

"I been thinking about that," Tiny drawled. The more he drawled, the heavier his thinking was. I'd long since noticed that.

Bits sighed. "I smell a sermon coming."

"Live with it." Tiny finished filling the dog food bowls for the raccoons and started pouring seed for the birds. "OK, we know that Jesus could feed five thousand people when He had to, right?"

"Right." I wondered where he was going or why that had anything to do with the woman.

"But He worked a lot with one person at a time too. A blind man here, a leper there. A woman. A girl. So it looked like He wasn't doing much. Our pastor said that His followers were expecting big things, huge important things, like take over the country and be king."

From near the refrigerator, Lynn called, "How many chickens should I cut up?"

"Three." Tiny continued, "And yet, that was how Jesus changed the world He lived in. With little things, one thing at a time."

"Not so little." Bits didn't look convinced. "Bringing Lazarus back to life wasn't so little."

"Yeah, but it was only one man, not the whole graveyardful. See what I mean? Individuals. Not whole crowds."

Lynn grinned. "My father says there's no

such thing as small potatoes. Enough potatoes make a truckload."

"There you are."

I thought about circumstantial evidence. Things that looked like they weren't related. Just little things. Unimportant things. But all together, they pointed a big finger of guilt at Mike and even at Bits and me.

I was developing a very healthy respect for little things.

Probably Bits was just trying to head Tiny off from preaching some more, but mostly she likes to argue. "OK, lots of little things. But if you don't have the really big things to go with all the little things, you got nothing."

"Well, yeah, but—" Tiny should have known better than to pick an argument with Bits.

She roared on, freight-train earnest. "Jesus never did a sin, but He paid for sin anyway. He gave His life when He shouldn't have, and He can use that to pay for our sins for us so that we don't have to. And since our sins are paid for, we can get into heaven, as long as we come to Him. Now, if you're gonna call that small potatoes—" she said that right at Lynn— "you're full of 'em! Potatoes, I mean."

Lynn raised both hands in a "who am I to argue?" gesture. She held a chicken leg in one hand and a knife in the other.

The phone rang, and Mike picked it up. He looked very tired—down-deep tired to the bone. He forgot he wasn't with his family, I guess, because he answered, *"Bueno,"* and quickly corrected himself. "I mean, Animal Rescue Facility, good morning. Uh-huh. OK. Here he is." He raised his voice. "Les?"

Who would be calling me? Feeling a little important, I walked over to him and took the cordless, even though he could have brought it to me. "Les Walker."

"It's me. Your dad. Are Lynn and Tiny there?"

"Yes, sir." I mouthed, *Dad*, to Lynn.

"Sergeant Ware and I were just talking to that mother who totaled her car. Jennifer Hughes is her name. She'd like us all to meet for lunch today. That includes Mike and Bits too. The whole Sugar Creek Gang."

"Uh, yeah, I guess. They close the place here from noon to one unless Tiny brings his lunch. So, yeah, I guess. Sure. OK."

"We'll pick you up around a quarter to twelve."

I said something brilliant, like, "Uh-huh," or, "Yeah, OK," again. I don't remember what. I pushed the hang-up button. "Ladies and gentlemen," I announced, "we are all about to meet a lady who has learned the hard way that little things can mean a lot."

23

When nicer ladies are invented, it's Mrs. Jennifer Hughes they're going to have to be nicer than. And now that her baby wasn't crying and choking on air bag powder, it was a cute little thing.

She said she wanted to take us all to lunch at our favorite restaurant. Dad and Sergeant Ware agreed that our favorite place was the Extraburger. In part, they said that because it's true. But mostly, I think, they didn't want her to have to pay out a whole lot of money, and the Extraburger, being your basic fast food place, doesn't drain your pockets as fast as some restaurants do.

Once, when I was a little kid, I decided that you could tell which people had accidents and which would get in trouble if you just knew the signs to look for. Sort of like you can tell which puppy in a litter is going to be the biggest dog. It will have the hugest, floppiest feet.

I'm about ready to give up that idea. It was just little-kid thinking anyway. There was nothing about Mrs. Hughes that would suggest she'd tune her radio at the wrong time, or forget about a stop sign in the neighborhood, or anything. She was normal.

And generous. She didn't have to include

Mike and Bits in the party, but she did. And then I learned why. One of our dads must have told her about the Sugar Creek Gang.

"Sugar Creek books? I grew up with them!" She laughed. "I'll tell you a secret. When I was your age, my parents made me read those books because they took place around here and because they're wholesome. I was a rebellious kid. I made my folks think I hated the books. The truth was, I loved them, but I didn't want to give Mom and Dad the satisfaction of knowing I did." She shrugged. "It was nuts. I was a nut when I was little. I know better now."

I glanced at Bits. If rebelling against your parents was a key to having accidents later, Bits was going to spend half her adult life in a body cast.

After the lunch, Sergeant Ware took Mike home to mow lawns all afternoon. Dad took Tiny, Lynn, Bits, and me to the shelter to get our bikes. We didn't go home right away, though. We helped Tiny clean cages first.

It took three times as long as I thought it would, and we worked pretty fast. Taking care of animals is a real chore. Finally, the four of us headed for our bikes. Tiny had put in his time and then some. There was a strict limit on how long kids could work there in a day.

And I thought, *Poor old Mike doesn't have any time limit.*

On the way home, Lynn called from behind me, "We should sit down and decide how much money we have and how much we need yet."

I turned to yell, "Mom was going to teach the girls how to make her chocolate chip cookies. If you don't mind some pretty weird cookies, come over to my house."

That idea was a hit. They all went home to get their financial records, so to speak, then they came to my place. An hour later, here we all were sitting around the dining room table. When Mom looked at us, I couldn't tell if she was really that dismayed or just acting like it. She sent Hannah to the store for more milk and sent us out to the half bath by the back door to wash our hands a couple times each. Actually, that wasn't such a bad idea.

And then we sat down with pencils to figure how much we had.

Tiny tried one of the less dark cookies. "We aren't going to have enough, because we got ten Dumpsters instead of twenty, but we should be close soon."

Bits dug into her pocket and dropped a tangled, crumpled wad of bills on the table. That girl had no respect for money.

Lynn frowned. "Where'd you get that? I thought you were going to buy the *Jungle Peril* upgrade."

"I decided not to."

I smirked. "I bet your dad said you weren't allowed to."

She glared at me, but then she softened. "My hard drive is too full. I don't have room for it."

I nodded. "So add more memory."

And then she confessed. "I wanted to, but Daddy said enough is enough."

Lynn punched Tiny's figures into her calculator, then mine, and hers. She uncrumpled Bits's savings, smoothing the bills out one by one. It was quite a stack, but they badly needed ironing, so I guess there wasn't as much there as it seemed.

Lynn did it over again. She asked each of us our figures, checking. She passed the calculator to Tiny. "Look."

Tiny's face twisted a moment, puzzled, then softened into the biggest, happiest grin. "I'll be dockered."

I frowned. "Dockered?"

"My granny always said that. Dunno what it means, but if she said it, it's OK. She didn't have to sneak into heaven through no back door. The angels was clamoring to invite her in."

Lynn smiled. "I like that. Live your life in such a way that the angels will clamor to let you into heaven. You're quite a poet, Tiny."

"Don't you never go saying that out in public! Hear?"

The smile did not fade in the least. "Of course not."

Tiny passed the calculator to Bits, and she handed it to me.

We were over the top.

We had it!

I whooped. We all did. You think angels can clamor? You should have heard us in that dining room, yelling and high-fiving.

Bits beamed. "We did it ourselves. We earned every penny of it, and nothing from our parents."

Tiny took the calculator from my hand and studied it. "You know how we did it? Sure, the Dumpster project gave us the chunk. But over half of it is nickel-and-dime stuff. A couple dollars here, a couple dollars there. It really adds up. That's what made the difference. The little things, saved steady."

I jumped up and ran out to the study. "Mom! Guess what!"

"You kids have enough for your bikes." She stood up, grinning. "They can hear you in Lake Oswego, you know." And then she engulfed me in one of those massive, crushing hugs she saves for only the most special of occasions.

Because it was.

24

How could we solve this dilemma?

Mike was a part of the gang, right? But Mike could not contribute to the price of the new bikes. He worked harder than anyone else, but he was helping support his family. That's an important thing, a really grown-up thing. So while he was earning family money, he was also earning our support and respect. Believe me, he was. But he was not earning a bike.

Now here's the problem. Do we invite him along to buy our bikes, since he's one of the gang and it's a gang thing? Or do we go get them without him? What would you do?

After supper that night, Dad headed for his study, so I followed him in and flopped into the wingback chair beside his recliner. I brought the problem up to him, explaining it in detail.

He cranked the handle on his recliner chair. It tipped back and shoved his feet up. "That's a problem, all right. What did you guys decide?"

"We didn't yet. Also, we're inviting you and Sergeant Ware and Mr. Wing to go along with us for the bikes since you guys were behind us and helped so much."

"We didn't do the work. You did."

"Yeah. But you greased the skids so we

could work. And you sort of paid attention so that we didn't mess up. Anyway, we decided that today."

"Well, thank you. I for one wouldn't miss it. Thanks for inviting me."

"You're welcome, but that doesn't solve our problem."

"True." He thought a few moments, his magazine lying open and unread on his lap. "What are your feelings?"

"I dunno."

"I'll put it this way: What would you like to do?"

"Take him along. He's one of us."

Dad nodded. "See? That's your feelings. You want to share the joy, and that's being thoughtful. Now, what would *his* feelings be, do you think? If you were he and he were you, how would you feel?"

I thought about that a little while. "Sad. I'd feel sad. Happy for my friends, but sad. Maybe even a little jealous."

"Does that solve your dilemma?"

"Yeah, I guess it does. His feelings come first, right?"

"That would be the best solution, yes."

Strike while the iron is hot, Mom always said. I had no idea what that really means, but I struck anyway. "OK, another question. When you're out to make money, like we were doing, how do you know if you're doing God's will?"

"Is that what the topical Bible and concordance were for?"

"Yeah. It didn't work."

He chuckled, deep and warm and throaty. "Do you know the difference between right and wrong?"

"Yeah, mostly."

"Do right. Avoid wrong. You'll be in God's will."

"No, I mean when you're making money, not just the general stuff."

"I'm not generalizing. When you're making money, do right. When you're not making money, do right. If your conscience bothers you, back off, whether you're making money or doing something else."

"I see." And I did see, but I couldn't explain it. I saw that making money wasn't a separate category in life. It was life. So was not making money. It didn't matter what you were doing or trying to do or not doing. You did the right thing, and that was God's will. The wrong thing wasn't. Period. And I'm still not explaining it well, but maybe you can see what I mean.

And then Dad relaxed. It was the neatest thing to watch, the way he would just sort of go limp. He would melt like a hot crayon into whatever he was sitting in. So here he was, draped like wet tissue paper in his chair, when the phone rang.

I jumped, but he never blinked. With a long, lazy swoop of the arm, he hit the button on the speaker phone on the desk beside him and said hello to the ceiling.

"Hello, Bill? Jim here." You could tell it was

Bits's dad by the sound of the voice. Not all speaker phones are that clear.

Dad didn't exactly un-relax, but he stiffened a bit, became more alert. "Good evening, Jim. What's up?"

"Quite a bit. I'm at the station yet. This afternoon, I talked to my lieutenant about our Detective Chase. Then I spent two hours talking to Chase himself. Now I'd like to bring him by for a few minutes, if I may."

Bring him here! I mouthed to Dad.

And Dad said, "Certainly."

If I had responded, I would have said, "I'd rather jam toothpicks under my fingernails than talk to Mr. Chase." But I wasn't the one on the phone.

Dad punched the button, closing the line. "Now, what's that all about?"

"You're asking me?"

He chuckled. "Why not? You know as much as I do."

They arrived about twenty minutes later. Mom answered the door, and Dad and I were standing up when she led them into the study. She took orders for coffee and left.

I could tell this time was different, because Mr. Chase shook hands with Dad and me both before he sat down in the wingback chair. He didn't do that before. Sergeant Ware swung around the desk chair to sit in. That left me with the footstool or nothing. So I chose nothing, hanging off the back of Dad's recliner to watch and listen.

Detective Chase began, "We've found the culprit in the fire at your church." He said it like fact, no bluffing this time.

My heart went thump. *Don't let it be Mike!* I prayed.

Mr. Chase looked at me. "Sergeant Ware here assisted me in finding your little friend Miguel Alvarado."

No! Please, God! I prayed harder.

"We also got a lead from Lieutenant Groves with the fire department and from your pastor, Mr. Earnhart." For some reason Mr. Chase acted very nervous and uncomfortable. "Following an intense investigation at the site and . . ." He started over. "To make a long story short, this is what happened:

"A cleaning woman in the back room of your church spilled some lamp oil when she was polishing a lamp, but she didn't take time just then to clean it up. She went off to take care of other duties and forgot about the spill."

I watched not Mr. Chase, but Sergeant Ware. He was studying the detective intently, as if trying to coach him along, pushing him into the right words to speak.

Detective Chase continued, "Late that afternoon, there was a wedding, with a lot of bustle in the back room, as you can imagine. We don't know exactly what happened next. Either the people cleaning up after the wedding were in a big hurry, or they were careless . . ."

I would vote for in a hurry, but then I'd only been to two weddings. At both of them, everyone behind the scenes ran around a lot without doing much.

Mr. Chase swallowed. "Somehow, when one of the candles used in the wedding ceremony was put aside, it wasn't quite out. Not fully extinguished. The wedding party left in a hurry. That candle kept burning and eventually ignited the spilled-oil stain."

It took a moment for all that to sink in. At first I didn't understand. And then, like a 300-watt light being turned on in a dark room, the truth flared up in me.

The fire was accidental! Mike had nothing to do with it!

Yahoo! Thank You, God! I didn't yell out loud, but my grin made my cheeks hurt.

Sergeant Ware sat back, looking relieved that this was over.

For a long moment, Dad blotted all this up. "It's clear to me, Detective, that you had assumed young Mike Alvarado's guilt. I suggest you owe him and his parents an apology."

"Sergeant Ware here and I went over there this afternoon and did just that."

"Good." Dad nodded. "Good."

Good! Thank You, Lord! Good. My heart sang like birds in spring.

Sergeant Ware sighed. "So that part is over. But the cleanup isn't, or the costs. If the woman who spilled the oil, or any of the people with the wedding, had just taken the proper care, it would never have happened."

I heard what he was saying. Little things.

25

It was here. The day we had all been waiting for had finally arrived.

Gormann Super Roadmaster time! Pinstripes and elegance, here we come!

Tiny and I rode over to Brookstone Mall with Dad. Lynn came with her father and Bits with hers. We had calculated the cost of four bikes to the penny, of course. With our careful saving and hard work—slave and save, Tiny called it—we had that amount and enough left over to treat the dads to lunch at the mall's food court.

The food court had nine different fast food places, from burgers through pizza to Chinese, plus a couple of dessert stands and a health food snack-and-sandwich place. We avoided that one, but between the seven of us, we hit most of the others. We scattered to choose our respective meals, then sat together at one of the big tables in the middle. It was the greatest time, with all of us laughing and talking.

Then came the *big moment*. We walked over to the bike shop and stepped inside.

The Gormann Super Roadmaster still leaned into its kickstand there in the window, the spotlights making its chrome dance and shine. We gathered around it, I in deep admiration, hoping the others admired it just as deeply.

Dad said, "I thought you were exaggerating when you described it, Les, but you weren't. Very nice."

Mr. Wing smiled. "Yes, and much more practical than I expected. It offers useful features."

Sergeant Ware nodded. "I like the safety features. The package is well thought out."

Said Bits, "I suppose I'll get a lot more use out of this than out of another computer game." There was a wistfulness in her voice, though, as if she wasn't quite sure that what she just said was true.

What now? I guessed one of us would announce to the salesman, "We'll take four of these, please." And I guessed that one would probably be me.

"Les?" Lynn stood apart from us a few feet. "Look over here."

"What?" I crossed to her. I can't explain it exactly, but somehow she was breaking the spell. That irritated me.

She pointed to a bicycle. "I know you have your heart set on the Gormann Super Roadmaster. And I'll be the first to agree it's an excellent bike. But look at this one.

She was pointing to the Gormann Roadmaster. Not Super. Not pinstriped. No water bottle. Ordinary tires. Plain blue without metallic fleck. This bike did not dazzle the way the other one did. Oh, sure, it was a good bike, with all the features you really needed, but it wasn't a *great* bike. Do you understand what I'm saying?

Of course, the plain old Roadmaster didn't cost as much as the other one, either. However, I couldn't see sacrificing elegance just to save a few bucks. I mean, there comes a time when you go for the gold and price take the hindmost (to quote my grandmother again).

Lynn whipped out that calculator of hers. "Here's the cost of the Super Roadmaster times four, right? With tax, of course. We already know that figure. And here's the cost of this Roadmaster times five."

Times five?

It took a moment, but then I caught on. "If we get this cheaper model, we can buy five bikes all alike. Mike can have one, too!"

You couldn't even hear us breathe, it was so quiet.

No! I wanted the great one! The Super one! I had been yearning for that bike so long.

And yet . . . and yet . . .

My heart slammed down on the ground, but then it lifted up and spread its wings again.

And yet . . .

I looked at Bits.

She thought a moment longer, then nodded. "Yeah. Let's do it."

I looked at Tiny.

He was grinning. "Can't you just see his face? I love it!"

Lynn studied her calculator. "We're a little

bit short of being able to buy five, but not much. Another week or two of kicking in part of our allowance should do it."

The three dads looked at each other. Sergeant Ware had some kind of emotion behind his face struggling to get out, and he was holding it in, his mouth tight. Mr. Wing's face melted into a sweet, gentle smile. He carefully studied the floor.

My dad's voice sounded a little husky. "How much are you short?"

"Eighteen dollars and thirty cents."

All three dads reached for their wallets.

Bits looked puzzled. "But, Daddy, you said you weren't going to help, remember?"

Her dad smiled. "I think this is worth it, Sugar. Mike needs a bike. Besides, it's just a little thing."

Moody Press, a ministry of Moody Bible Institute,
is designed for education, evangelization, and edification.
If we may assist you in knowing more about Christ
and the Christian life, please write us without obligation:
Moody Press, c/o MLM, Chicago, Illinois 60610.